Shadow on
Mercer Mountain

Shadow on
Mercer Mountain

Daoma Winston

PIATKUS

This edition first published in
Great Britain in 1988 by
Judy Piatkus (Publishers) Ltd of
5 Windmill Street, London W1
by arrangement with
Abner Stein Agency, London SW7

British Library Cataloguing in Publication Data
Winston, Daoma, *1922–*
    Shadow on Mercer Mountain.
    I. Title
    813′.54[F]

ISBN 0–86188–752–2

Printed and bound in Great Britain by
Mackays of Chatham PLC, Chatham, Kent

Chapter 1

"THAT MAN at the throttle," the plump steward grinned, "he's calling you all kinds of names right now. And none of them nice either. He don't stop here, not ever, unless he has to. And when he does, then it's a long, slow haul up the big hill. You'll see. You'll find out just what I mean in a minute. So get yourself ready now."

The steward had Jan Olney braced and waiting. The platform door was open, and the chill of the pre-dawn air blew pleasantly on her flushed cheeks, and tousled her dark curls. Even so, the train paused so briefly he barely had time to swing her bags off and Jan with them before the big wheels began to grind faster, and the cars to jostle each other, and the laboring engine began its first ascent to the unseen pass.

With the light, the heat, the clatter retreating slowly, then more quickly, then gone, Jan was completely alone. Alone in a swift heavy silence that was underscored by the faint sounds of the vibrating hum in the tracks behind her.

She looked first at the sky, where, to the east, rimming a flat distant horizon, a pale blur of pink promised that the sun would soon rise. Then she looked at the tiny station. It was no more than a single rectangular shadow at the edge of nothing, a greater depth of dark against the dark that surrounded it. There was no light, not a bulb burning, no sound, not a whisper of movement.

She jerked a small blue cloche over her dark curls and buttoned the matching blue coat she wore. She stood there, hesitating, and then, because there was nothing else to do, she picked up her bags, and went toward the station, and on around it. There, she stopped to look toward the faint blur of pink on the horizon.

7

In that direction was home, routine, friends. The security of the familiar, the known. She sighed, and straightened her shoulders, and resolutely turned her back on it. She had come that far, deliberately, to consider the unfamiliar, the unknown.

Facing the station again, she realized that the pink blur had spread, and that now the shadows had acquired edges and form. And one of those forms, she decided, was that of a parked car.

She thought that anywhere else in the world she could assume that the car would be a taxi, that somewhere nearby, though where she couldn't imagine, she would find its driver.

But there, in Mercer, on the edge of the great mountain ranges, she dared make no such assumption. Still, stumbling with the weight of the bags, she went toward the car. As she did, a door snapped open.

A man, tall and lean, but faceless in the almost-dark, got out, yawned, stretched widely, and then demanded, "Miss Olney? Is that you?"

"Yes," she said. "I'm Jan Olney."

The man, still faceless, leaned down toward her. "Of course," he said. "Who else could you be? David's fine bones, his eyes. . ."

Her wound was still too fresh to be covered with anything but the most brief courtesy. She said into a momentary silence, "And you are . . . ?"

"Bill Edwards. I worked with David at the Consulate."

"You worked with David?" Jan echoed. "You knew him? I don't recognize your name."

"I'm not surprised he didn't write about me. It was a casual acquaintance." Then, in a deep, sincere voice, "I don't have to tell you, do I? I'm sorry about what happened."

Again brief courtesy had to suffice. She thanked him, her stiff lips barely moving with the words.

He picked up her bags and said, "I hope you didn't stand around here waiting too long. I'm afraid I dozed off."

"I'm glad there was someone to meet me. I wondered how I'd get out to the house."

"But what did you think? Of course there would be someone to meet you. She was glad, over-joyed, I should say, when your letter arrived. She . . ."

"Ellen was?"

"Certainly. And as for meeeting you . . . they aren't savages after all."

Fortunately, Jan didn't have to answer that. Else she might have told him that she had any number of reasons to think that the Ballantines, if not he himself, were savages. But the train whistle suddenly moaned, a hoarse, single-note wail that made her shiver. She raised her head, listening.

The dark had thinned, turned blue. Now she could see Bill's face. He had a big, almost hooked nose, a predatory nose, she thought. Deep set dark eyes peered from under flaring black brows. His cheekbones were high, the flesh under them hollowed, his mouth peculiarly long, and now turned down in a grin that was full of strange sudden awareness.

"You think that's a nice sound, do you?"

"I do," Jan agreed.

"You're a different generation from me then. I like the old-fashioned ones. The steam whistles. A long, long cry, with enough juice to it for a half hour echo."

She didn't answer him. She judged him to be about thirty, which put them in the same generation. She wondered suddenly where he had grown up.

He said, "You're younger than I thought somehow. I don't know why."

Again she didn't answer him.

He gave a faint sigh, still leaning toward her, and then he shrugged, "Ready then?"

But she didn't move until the single-note wail had died away, leaving nothing more than a faint humming, a displacement in the still air. At last, she nodded.

He went ahead to the car, taking long strides, and swinging her bags so easily that they might have been filled with tissue paper. He stowed them in the trunk and helped her into the front seat.

She wondered why, if David had known him, if they had really worked together, she had never heard his name before.

Bill Edwards.

Who was he?

Not that it was really impossible that David had had a friend about whom he hadn't written. Rather it was quite probable. Yet, where had Bill been during David's illness? If they had worked together, were friends, even casual acquaintances, why had he not been with David then? And why, why was he here now?

"Self-sufficient," Bill said suddenly. "That's what I'd always heard." Something in the way he ground the gears as he got the car into motion gave the remark an edge of disapproval. "I guess that's why I expected you to be older."

"It was the way we were brought up," she told him. "The way we lived. We were alone, you know. Separated, and in school, a good deal of the time. And even when we travelled together . . ."

"I know," Bill said. "Your father was a very busy man, wasn't he?"

"There were so many things . . . all over the world . . . once he was in them . . ."

"But how old are you? I mean really . . . self-sufficiency and all."

She heard the sound of laughter in his deep voice, and glanced at him. But his face was sober, noncommittal. She had the feeling that its lack of expression was for her benefit.

She answered, "I'm twenty-three." In her own voice there was something tired, something hurt. She recognized it, went on briskly, "Yes. Twenty-three a few months ago."

"A nice round number of years." Now he slid a quick sideways glance at her. "I expected you to be older, I told you that, and yet, when I saw you, I thought you were younger." He grinned then. "You don't look twenty-three, forgive me."

She turned her face to the window. The morning breeze brushed her hot cheeks like quick cool fingers. A deep blue light spread over waist-high pampas grass.

"It's no crime, for a woman, to look young," Bill said softly. "Don't be sad about it." He added, "And besides not being a crime, it's sometimes a very great advantage."

She straightened her hat with a slow deliberate motion, and then, just as deliberately, she turned and looked at him. "What do you mean, Mr. Edwards? What do you *really* mean?"

He gave her a pained look. "Please. Please. I told you I knew David."

"Bill, then."

"Thank you, Janine."

Her heart gave a small leap. No one ever called her that. No one. Least of all David.

But Bill repeated it, lingering over the syllables. And he laughed softly. "Yes. I can see why it was shortened to Jan. Of course. I can see that."

So her heart's small leap meant nothing at all. He had known that she was always called Jan, so perhaps he had known David. Perhaps everything Bill had said, everything of the little he had said, was true.

Yet she wondered why he was here, at the Ballantines'. She wondered how long he had been with them.

Small questions beside the larger ones.

What's happening to Ellen? David had cried, sweating with fever, his eyes too bright, his lips parched, dry, no matter how much water Jan gave him to sip.

Why doesn't she come?

What's wrong with her?

What do her letters mean, Jan?

And again, *What's happening to Ellen?*

Jan had promised him, promised him that she would find out. She would go to Ellen. She would answer the summons for help that David could not then answer himself. That, though he didn't know it, never knew it, he would never be able to answer himself.

Jan blinked away tears, asked, "But what did you mean? and the way you said it, too? that it's an advantage to look younger?"

"It's disarming," Bill said. "Very disarming. Which comes in handy sometimes."

She turned to look at him.

He was staring at the winding road ahead, mouth stern. The momentary teasing laughter was stilled. He looked sober, intent, and somehow, in a way she couldn't define, oddly dangerous.

"You're wondering what I'm doing here, aren't you?" he asked.

She had been, of course, and so, making the denial that tact required, she faltered, murmured, "Well, I suppose there *are* things . . ."

"I was on leave, home leave, when it happened, Jan. That's why we didn't meet when you were there. We would have otherwise. I'm sure of that. But anyway, since I was in the country, and since I knew Ellen . . ."

"You *knew* her?"

"Certainly. Why not? We're just a small group out there. Naturally I met her. Oh, not often. They were still honeymooners for one thing." He stopped for a moment. He sighed, then went on, "And David . . . well, you know that he wasn't an out-going person, so . . ." Bill shrugged. "Of course, very soon, Ellen went home, and . . ."

"And didn't return."

Bill nodded. "And after David died, there were certain formalities."

"I know that. I took care of them," Jan said, and blinked again against sudden hot tears.

"Yes. But you're David's sister. Those things that you had to do, still have to do, I suppose, else why are you here? Those things are concerned with his life as your brother, as your father's son. But the forms, the insurance, the annuity, all that, concerns Ellen, only Ellen, because she was David's wife."

Jan nodded.

"So I drove down, down from Denver where I was

staying. I arrived two days ago. It didn't take long to turn over the papers. Only moments actually. But I've stayed on. It seemed to do Ellen good."

It was, Jan thought, very kind of him to be concerned about Ellen, to care how David's widow fared, to remain beyond the time required by what he had described as a few moments of official business. It was certainly thoughtful, yet Jan, still feeling that he was somehow dangerous, didn't believe him.

"I'm looking forward to seeing Ellen," Jan said. "And the whole family, of course."

"You'll find her somewhat changed, I'm afraid. I hardly recognized her myself."

"But I've never seen Ellen," Jan said expressionlessly. "Not her nor any of the Ballantines, for that matter."

"Oh, yes of course. They did not tell me that." Then, "And it's been an ordeal for Ellen, all of it, you know. The worst was not being able to go to David."

It had been, Jan thought, an ordeal for David, too.

A bride, cherished for three, or had it been four months? Then six months of hungering loneliness. And then . . .

Bill went on, a rasp in his voice. "There. Mercer. What there is of it anyway."

She followed the gesture of his lean hand. The narrow macadam road spun past signs, a huddle of buildings that rose out of pink sunrise, dusty she-oak trees, a horse trough at the edge of a small square. And in the center of the square . . .

Jan's gray eyes widened. "What on earth is that?"

"Barely on earth," Bill laughed. "You're looking at the Mercer Monster. A thing of wood, tin, paint, I don't know what else."

She turned, looking back as they drove by. The Mercer Monster stood ten feet tall, carved out of a single huge log. A face, tin hammered into the wood for eyes, for nose, for mouth. A hat made of tin. Red shirt with metal buttons. Blue trousers with a metal belt buckle. Steel spikes, nail heads, brass studs, bits of glass. All those had been beaten into the splintering wood.

"It's a totem from the old days," Bill explained. "When there was gold in the hills, gold on Mercer Mountain. Somebody put it up then. It began as a joke. A man made a strike and left a nugget in the skin of the Mércer Monster. Other men did the same. It was supposed to be for good luck."

"There's no gold in him now," she said.

"Not any more. Just tin, rusty nails, bits of glass."

"A monument to greed." She turned in her seat. "It's as ugly to look at as what it stands for."

"The tourists find it charming," Bill told her. "And there's little else in town. But . . ." he nodded, "straight ahead is Mercer Mountain."

It was the first sharp, jutting thrust at the edge of the western range. Before it lay miles of pink-touched meadow. It reared its peak from dusky red shadows.

"And that's where we're going. You can't see the Ballantine lodge yet, but in a little while you'll get a glimpse of it."

She looked at Mercer Mountain, rock and ridges and stands of cedar, all still enwrapped in dusky red shadow. She suddenly felt the chill of the early morning, and shivered, and drew her coat more closely around her.

"You'll be warm soon," he said. "The sun is like fire here. And you'll have some coffee, a decent breakfast, as soon as we get there. It will make you feel like yourself again."

She smiled faintly. "Thank *you* for *your* hospitality."

He caught the edge of sarcasm, and reacted in a way that took her aback.

A frown cut a gouge between his dark brows. Hard lines put brackets around his mouth. He whipped the car to the side of the road and slammed on the brakes.

Chapter 2

THERE WAS impatience in the way he turned in the seat, in the way his dark eyes narrowed.

She didn't know what to expect. She felt herself go tense.

But finally, in a soft voice, he said, "Look, Jan, we'd better talk about this. You've got the wrong idea completely."

"Have I?" she murmured.

"Obviously. You're coming here with your hackles up. You're hurt, for David's sake. I can understand that. But it wasn't the way you think. It wasn't indifference. It wasn't cruelty. Please believe me. You're welcome, and more than welcome here. I know, I had just arrived when your letter came. I saw Ellen's reaction with my own eyes. She was happy, and excited."

Jan managed to keep her face expressionless. Ellen happy?

Well, perhaps. Perhaps Bill's choice of words had been a poor one. He might have meant that Ellen was relieved. That would make sense. Ellen might easily be relieved to know that Jan bore her no animosity for what had happened, relieved to know that Jan was coming.

But why was Ellen surprised?

She had herself sent those three frantic letters begging David to come, to help her. Help her how? In what way? What was wrong? Why, when she knew that David could not, must not, leave his post, had she begged him to? Why had his cables gone unanswered? Why had he never been able to reach her by long-distance phone?

David, sinking into fever, had moaned the questions in thin whispers. Jan, leaning to him, had promised, in

15

almost the last words he could ever have heard, that she would go to Ellen.

The day David fell ill, he had been packed, awaiting only a plane reservation to answer Ellen's pleas, his own to her having failed. The Consulate notified Ellen of his collapse, and had been told that she would start out at once to join him. Within a few hours, the cable telling of her breakdown arrived. Then, and only then, Jan was called. David died three days later, his brilliant promise unfulfilled, his sweetness a light gone out of the world forever.

Jan had called Ellen and had spoken the most difficult words she had ever had to speak. It was then, remembering her promise to David, that Jan told Ellen that she would visit her soon. And three weeks later, Jan had written, giving the day, the date, the time, of her arrival.

So why was Ellen surprised?

Bill was saying, "Listen, Jan, if it's because none of the Ballantines came to meet you . . . well, I'd better explain about that. It's my fault actually. I wanted to see you first. First and alone."

"Is that so?" She turned to look at him. "And why?"

There was a sudden grimness around his mouth. "Let's say I wanted to prepare you."

She matched his grimness. "Let's say I don't believe you."

He ignored that. "And I wanted to know how you feel, what you think."

She eyed him, waiting.

"The situation being what it is . . ." He shrugged his wide shoulders. "You might have the idea . . ." Then, "And I was right."

She said evenly, "You mean that I might feel some small resentment, don't you?"

"You were very close to David, weren't you?"

She smiled, a sudden warm smile that put a glow into her gray eyes and lightened them to silver. "Close. Yes." Her smile deepened. Dimples suddenly appeared in her cheeks. "Very close. Even though we were both so self-sufficient." But then the sudden smile, the dimples, faded.

She said, "I don't think that I blame Ellen. I wish it had been different. I know that it ought to have been different. But I don't think I blame her."

"I'm glad to hear it. I suppose, more than anything, that's what I wanted to know." Bill started the car, swung it back on the highway. "Sometimes, under such strange circumstances, people *do* get odd ideas, you know."

She was listening, suspicion sharpening her intuition as well as her ears. She caught, yes she was sure of it, a note of relief in his words. But she said only, "These circumstances don't occur very often."

He agreed. Then, "Of course, when Ellen's sister Thalia fell ill, and the family sent for Ellen, she felt she had to come home. And then, when poor Thalia died, Ellen took it so hard."

Jan felt Bill's dark eyes on her face, a swift searching glance that had a question in it.

Jan asked, "How is Ellen now?"

"You can imagine." His voice was sober. "I understand that she was much improved, but that when David died, I'm sorry, Jan, she had a relapse. If she could have gone to David, been with him, as you were, she'd be better for it, you know."

"Exactly what was wrong?" Jan asked, keeping her voice steady.

"Don't you know?"

"No details. Just that she was ill, couldn't speak on the phone, and couldn't come."

But Jan thought of the letters again. She thought of them and didn't mention them. Why? She wasn't sure. Except that Ellen had been afraid, had pleaded for help.

Bill was saying, "I guess they didn't want to worry David. And then, let's face it, even in this day and age, plenty of people have an old-fashioned idea about . . ." He sighed. "Ellen had a breakdown of some kind after Thalia died. They were just a few years apart in age, Ellen twenty-one, Thalia twenty-three. It was an intense relationship, I've gathered."

"You've gathered a great deal in two days, haven't you?" Jan said thoughtfully.

"I wanted to know." He went on. "Ellen went down, fading. Blank spaces in her memory. A blackout of all kinds of things big and small. The Ballantines did everything they could. And she's coming out of it again now. But the relapse was very serious. She's changed a great deal."

"Of course."

Once again his dark eyes slid sideways in a searching glance. "I suppose, though you've never met any of them, you must know a great deal about the Ballantines."

"Very little in fact. David didn't have much to say, except about Ellen."

"They're an unusual family."

"Close," Jan said, her voice dry. "Very close, aren't they?"

"You insist on holding that question against me, don't you?"

"Not really." Her sudden warm smile, her dimples, appeared briefly and faded.

"You do have business with Ellen? That's why you're here?"

Jan nodded, and a curl broke free of her small blue cloche hat. She smoothed the dark shining strands, and tucked them away. Her gray eyes, suddenly reflecting the color of the cedar through which they were passing, turned a shadowy dull green as she looked thoughtfully ahead.

"Surely it's the sort of thing that could have been handled by mail."

"Yes," she said, then stopped, expecting that he would bluntly ask her why, if that were true, she had made the trip, and wondering just what answer she could give him.

Instead he asked, "Is it very complicated stuff? I mean . . . will it take much time?"

"Much time? Oh, I don't know. As much time as it has to. There really isn't any hurry."

"Just papers to sign . . ." Bill paused. "I realize, of course, that there's a great deal involved. But . . ."

"But what?"

"I hope you won't have to stay long, Jan."

"I'll stay as long as I must," she said, but she wasn't thinking of the estate David had left, the properties, stocks, bonds, willed to Ellen, but over which Jan, as his executor, had to preside.

"It's a big job for anyone as young as you."

"I've done it before."

"Your father, you mean."

She nodded.

"I hope you can handle it quickly."

"So you've said. But why?"

He hesitated. Then, "It wouldn't be good for you, now, after what's happened, to spend too much time here."

It was a gentle remark, considerate. Yet it struck her as too facile to be the truth.

He had come with papers to be signed, done what he had to do, and lingered on. But he didn't want her there. She wondered why.

She looked thoughtfully ahead. As she watched, the dusky red shade slowly faded, gave way to the thrust of the bright, biting sun at their backs.

They followed a hairpin curve, slowed for a turn, and there, above them, on a gray ridge, the redwood wings of the big house glowed in the morning light with the color of blood.

He said, in a big brother voice, faintly reminiscent of David, "You should get away as soon as you can. Take a trip. Visit with relatives. Just forget everything that's happened."

"I've done all the traveling I want to. I have no relatives. And I don't want to forget my brother," she answered softly, and then, just as softly, asked, "How long will you be staying, Bill?"

It was a challenge. She was certain that he recognized it as such.

But he grinned. "I don't know. I've got months left of my home leave, you know. And I don't have any special place to go."

He pulled into a parking area at the foot of a steep flight of stone steps. There was another car there, a huge black limousine, its glistening chrome and paint dulled by a layer of pink dust.

"Ballantine Lodge," Bill told her, gesturing toward the stone steps. And then, following her eyes toward the limousine, "Oh, yes, they do nicely."

The huge redwood house she had glimpsed from below . . .

The expensive black limousine . . .

The Ballantines obviously had wealth, Jan thought. It was something to remember..

But she said aloud, "Thanks for meeting me, Bill."

"My pleasure, Jan." He smiled at her, unexpected warmth in his dark eyes, in his long, turned-down mouth, as if that had truly been his only motive. Then, he said, "They'll all be up, waiting for you, of course." When Jan didn't reply, he added, "There'll be a lot to talk about."

"But no real rush. I don't want to make it hard on Ellen."

There was no real rush. But it wasn't for the reason Jan had just given Bill. She would put no time limit to her visit. The talk, the papers, the transfers, everything could, and must wait until Jan understood what Ellen's letters had meant. Why she had pleaded for David to come to her. Why she had begged for his help.

Bill cut the ignition, then turned sideways, looking thoughtfully at Jan. "I wish you had waited a little longer before coming."

"But why?" The question was automatic. She had expected no answer, and received none.

He got out, took her bags from the trunk. He looked sober, intent again, and once more, oddly dangerous.

She followed him to the foot of the steep stone steps. He moved aside, motioned her ahead of him.

She climbed slowly, clutching her small blue purse, eyes fixed on the redwood wings, the huge glass windows that she knew must offer a breath-taking view, on the walled edge of the terrace just visible at the gray ridge.

David had sent her pictures. Pictures of Ellen and

Thalia. Pictures of Ian and Carl. The background the Coliseum, Caracula's baths. Hadrian's tomb. The Spanish Steps, where David and Ellen had met. Romantic Rome, a perfect setting for swift, sweet, tragic love.

Memory of those pictures fell like spinning leaves through Jan's mind.

Young, glowing, golden-haired Ellen.

Joyful David . . .

Bill seemed to be at Jan's heels, almost but not quite, hurrying her. "Remember. Ellen's changed."

Still, when Jan reached the last step, went beyond it onto the terrace, she wasn't prepared.

She stood there, small, slender, vulnerable, her heart-shaped face blank, her curved lips frozen, her silver eyes wide with bewilderment.

Dwarfed by Bill, who stood just behind her, by the big house, and the mountain beyond it, she looked like a lost child, a frightened child. And, like a frightened child, she shivered in the bright, hot early sunlight.

Bill exhaled an audible sigh.

Jan braced herself, and made herself smile.

The girl who waited in the open doorway wore black, mourning black. Her hair was long, golden. Her face was thin, haggard. Her wide blue eyes glistened with tears.

Ellen.

It had to be Ellen.

She cried, "Jan, oh, Jan, I'm so glad to see you," and came forward slowly, her long hair flowing like molten gold around her narrow shoulders, her slim white hands out, reaching.

Just as slowly, Jan went to meet her.

And, in movement, in unwilling movement, propelled forward by conscious effort, Jan swallowed the words on her lips, wiped the words from her mind.

Still, an echo remained, a whisper, a trailing fear, and as she took the girl into her arms, the pictures drifted through her memory again, and she thought, You're not Ellen! You can't be Ellen!

The girl, answering Jan's unspoken cry, murmured hoarsely, "Oh, I know, I know. I'm changed so much, Jan. You must wonder that David ever loved me!" and began to weep.

Chapter 3

JAN HELD the thin, drooping body, smoothed the golden hair on the wet cheek, whispered out of a throat constricted by sympathy, "Ellen, Ellen dear it's all right . . ." and looked for aid to the man who had followed Ellen out of the house. Her older brother Ian, Jan knew.

Ian Ballantine.

Jan always remembered how he looked then. Big, hard as the ridges of Mercer Mountain, immobile as the ridges of Mercer Mountain.

He, like Ellen, was blond, but his hair was shot through with red, and glowed, as if touched by fire, in the sun. It was cut short, yet lay in smooth, full waves against his big head. His eyes, set deep under thick reddish brows, were like fire, too, hot blue flame dancing in the craggy planes of his face. He was taller even than Bill, at least six foot four, and built to that height, with a great barrel chest and wide thick shoulders.

For a moment, he was still, squinting into the sunlight, as if he were prolonging the scene. Ellen weeping in Jan's arms . . .

Jan always remembered that, too.

But then, finally, he mqved, and came forward, and as he took Ellen from Jan, he murmured formally, "I am very sorry, Miss Olney. Forgive us this welcome. I had hoped that my poor sister . . ."

Jan cried, "Oh, please, please don't . . ."

But his blue flame eyes looked past her to Bill. "Would you?"

Bill said, "Take her inside, Ian."

Ian, with another blue flame glance at Jan, swept

23

Ellen up into his arms. She was as limp as a broken doll as he carried her into the house.

Bill stood close to Jan, his lean body towering over her.

She listened as Ellen's cries receded, then faded away completely.

In the sudden silence that followed, Jan heard a sweet trill, and looked up to see a blue and white bird, its wings spread, go soaring upward from the silvered cedar roof.

"I was afraid of that," Bill said quietly. "But I'd hoped . . ."

"She has her memories," Jan answered.

"I'm glad you understand."

"You must have expected me to be made of stone," she said evenly, "to think that I might not understand."

He denied that quickly, yet she was aware that his dark eyes were narrowed, searching her face.

She turned away from him, a small underground river of distrust that was already suddenly deepening in her.

Who was Bill Edwards?

What was he doing here?

He said now, "Let's go in, Jan. I'll get you that coffee and breakfast I promised you."

Following him inside, she asked, "And the others, Bill?"

"The others?" He hesitated. Then, "Well, of course, Carl, the younger brother, is away at school. I assumed you knew that." He went on at her nod. "And you probably know, too, that Mrs. Ballantine is an invalid."

"David did say something about that. He didn't know her, of course. She wasn't able to go abroad with the rest of the family, so . . ."

"You'll meet her later," Bill cut in quickly.

"Of course," Jan agreed. "Later."

They stepped from sunlight into shadow.

The house was absolutely still.

Jan paused in the foyer, listening to the quality of the silence, as if it could, with its own language, speak to her.

Bill said, in a voice that seemed much too loud, "I'll

find Mrs. Mayor, the housekeeper. She'll take you up to your room." He left Jan s bag in the corner, gave her a swift, empty smile, and disappeared through a side door.

Alone, Jan looked around.

The foyer was big, starkly barren. Off to her right was an arched doorway. Beyond it she saw a long wide living room. It had a fireplace that covered one wall. The huge floor-to-ceiling windows that she had seen from outside formed another.

The wide expanse of uncarpeted oak floor gleamed with polish. The few pieces of furniture, a sofa, three chairs, a few tables, were obviously expensive. Yet the room looked peculiarly unlived in. There were no pictures, none of the bric-a-brac that reveals the character of the family which chooses, saves, and places it. The absence of personality seemed to indicate transience. Jan suddenly wondered how long the Ballantines had actually lived in the lodge.

Mrs. Mayor, a small, plump woman, whose round blue eyes shone brightly from a round, wrinkled face, came bustling in, and swept Jan, with Bill trailing them, up a short flight of steps, and down a long hall.

Beginning the moment that Bill introduced her to Jan, Mrs. Mayor spoke and didn't stop. The words bounced out of her plump face in the same quick rhythm of her plump feet.

"I'm so glad to see you," she said, smiling. "We need some brightness in this house, we do." She covered, without waiting for any reply, the weather, the scenery, and life. And finally, at their destination, breathless before a wide door, she said, "And here we are. At your room. All ready for you, I must say. Now you'll want a wash, and then, when you are settled, do come down." She flung the door open. "Step in. Yes, do. I'll go along and expect you soon." Retreating backward down the hall, she added, "Did you have a good trip?"

Bill grinned, put Jan's bags down just inside the door. "She's something, isn't she?"

"Non-stop good will," Jan said, and asked carefully, "But what about Sarah Jarvis?"

"Sarah Jarvis?"

"The woman that raised Ellen, the others."

"I don't know." Bill's grin was quite gone. "What about her?"

"David mentioned her. She was with Ellen and Thalia on the trip . . ."

"Perhaps she no longer works for them," Bill said. "I've never heard the name." He turned toward the door. "See you downstairs then?"

She nodded. She stood still, listening as his footsteps receded until she could no longer hear them, nor anything else. Until, once again, the strange whispering silence seemed to enwrap the house, speaking to her in a language she couldn't quite understand.

She told herself that it was a faculty of mind to invest a place with the quality of those things that had happened there. Thalia had died in the house, and Ellen had wept there, and so it was here that Jan listened to a whispering silence.

With an uneasy shrug, she looked around.

The room was pleasant, bright with sun that streamed through huge windows draped in blue.

The mahogany furniture was waxed, well-cared for. The big mirror sparkled.

But she found herself tiptoeing as she went to the closet to hang her coat, and tiptoeing still as she unpacked.

With that chore finished, as settled as she thought she had to be, she went to the window.

The view, facing east, was of great sprawling meadows that stretched from the base of Mercer Mountain. Meadows which, though brilliant with sunlight, were as desolate as the room itself.

She had been prepared. She had not come blindly to visit the Ballantines. Yet now, as she listened to the shrouding silence, she was cold. Cold with a fear she didn't understand. And she wondered, after all, why she had come, if she had been right to come. But even in that questioning moment, she knew the answer . . . .

She didn't remember her mother. There had always

been just the three of them. Her father Steven, a big, bald-headed man with the nose that was an eagle's beak, and with an eagle's far-seeing eyes. Her brother David, five years older than she was, big, too, with dark curls, and a straight gray gaze. And Jan herself. The three of them.

She loved her father and David with an intensity that never faltered through separation or growing up. Steven, ambitious in spite of inherited wealth, had far-flung interests. David and Jan always traveled with him, tutored by private teachers, until first David, later Jan, were both enrolled in school. From then on, they gathered only during vacation periods, months when the familial bonds were reinforced, when they knew love without dependency, without demands.

David, fulfilling Steven's hopes, had gone to Georgetown University, graduated from the School of Foreign Service, and immediately took a job in the State Department. He was posted to a Consulate in Buenos Aires, promoted from there to Alexandria, then transferred to Beirut.

Jan completed studies at Bennington, prepared to settle in New York. It was then, when she was twenty-one, that Steven died suddenly, leaving his fortune divided between her and David.

She saw David only twice, both times briefly, in the next two years, when he returned, on orders, to the United States. A little less than a year before, he had written joyfully of his marriage to Ellen. He described the romantic meeting on the Spanish Steps in Rome. Ellen and Thalia, chaperoned by Sarah Jarvis, the woman who had taken care of them, their mother being an invalid, had been nervously waiting to meet Ian and Carl. David, with the informality of an American to other Americans in foreign cities, had spoken first to Thalia, but soon turned to Ellen, and almost immediately had fallen in love with her. With his mission in Rome completed, he had married her and taken her back to Beirut. The rest of the family had returned home, and, David said, would, when they arrived in New York, get in touch with Jan.

He had sent pictures in that first letter, pictures that served as her first introduction to the Ballantines. Ellen, slim, blonde, dimpled, glowing with joy. Her sister Thalia, just a year older, blonde, too, but somehow withdrawn, with her eyes shadowed. Carl, about seventeen, slight, and grinning. And big Ian, somewhere in his middle thirties, towering over the others. Those pictures . . . Jan's first introduction to the Ballantines, and the only one until she came to the house in the shadow of Mercer Mountain.

Though David had written that they would get in touch with her as soon as they arrived in New York, she had never heard from them. And, after David's first letter, which also invited her to visit him and Ellen in Beirut, she didn't hear from him. She decided to give him and his new wife time to settle down together, so it was four months before she wrote to say she would like to see them.

David answered, suggesting that Jan wait a little while, since Ellen had returned home to visit with Thalia, who had been ill. Nearly five months later, Jan had the call that brought her to Beirut. She found David in a desperate condition. Weakened by fever, sinking, only rational for moments at a time, he managed to tell her about his attempts to call Ellen, about her pleading letters, about the cable explaining her collapse. Before he died, Jan promised him that she would go to Ellen . . .

Now, three weeks later, looking at the sunbright meadows that seemed so desolate to her, she sighed, remembering that promise. She must, for David's sake, learn the truth. Yet her every instinct warned her to leave the Ballantine house at once.

There were too many things she didn't understand.

Who was Bill Edwards? What was he doing there? Why if he had been a friend of David, even a casual one, had she never heard of him? Why had he wanted to see her first, and alone? Why had he suggested that she make her visit short?

There were easy answers, of course. She knew them. David wouldn't have mentioned everyone he knew in

Beirut. Bill, on home leave, had been asked by the Consulate, as he said, to attend to some business details for Ellen. He had wanted to see Jan first so that she wouldn't evince too much surprise, too much shock, at Ellen's pathetic condition. Easy answers, yes. But somehow they didn't satisfy Jan.

And Ellen . . .

Jan remembered the initial impression she had had, the sense that the frail blonde girl in the doorway could not be Ellen.

Jan knew she must be wrong. Illness, the shock of David's death, had left Ellen changed so that the pictures of the gay, smiling girl seemed to be of someone else. And yet . . . ?

Jan sighed again, then leaned forward.

Below her, on the rim of the terrace, she saw a shadow move in the sunlight. Bill appeared there, stood with his head down, his hands in his pockets, looking, it seemed to her, at the view she had herself just been studying. His immobility was that of a poised hunter. He turned then, as if speaking to someone. The sun was on his face. His taut body seemed to relax, sag. He grinned.

She backed away from the window.

It was as if she had watched him change, change in an instant, from one man to another. From a poised hunter, purposeful, dangerous, to . . . to what? She couldn't define the difference, but it was there. She knew only that Bill was part of *it*, whatever *it* was. She would have to watch him, to watch him as well as the others.

Hurrying now, she showered, brushed her dark curls, put on a narrow white shift. As she gave herself a quick final glance in the mirror, she noticed the big file she had brought with her. It was heavy, containing, neatly arranged, all those documents which would make Ellen heir to David's half of the Olney fortune, containing also David's letters from Beirut, and the pictures he had sent Jan.

She took the file, set it on the closet shelf, telling herself that before she took it down again, she would know the answers to David's questions.

What's happening to Ellen?
Why doesn't she come?
What do her letters mean, Jan?

Jan looked, for a moment, at the sprawling meadows. That way, easterly, was the security of the familiar, the known. She straightened her slim shoulders, and turned away.

Hand on the door knob, she hesitated.

There were faint sounds in the hall, no more than two quick breaths, then the whisper of retreating movement.

She waited until the faint sounds were gone, then she opened the door and went out.

Chapter 4

THE LONG HALL was empty, the door across from hers, the door at its end, firmly closed. Yet, as Jan turned toward the stairs, she felt as if unseen eyes watched her.

She wondered if Mrs. Mayor could possibly have been eavesdropping, then retreated behind one of the closed doors to peer at her.

But, when she descended into the foyer, Mrs. Mayor bounced to meet her, crying, "Miss Olney, oh, that is so formal, may I call you Jan?" and with Jan's smiling assent, rushed on, "Oh, Jan dear, do go into the big room. Just to your left there. The gentlemen are waiting for you. And I'll be just a moment with the coffee. And, when you've caught your breath, why, then do come along to the terrace. I've set up there. Such a lovely day, and the view . . . Oh . . ." Her blue eyes beamed in her round face. "It's so lovely to have you here."

Jan's thanks caused the smallest break in the bouncing words. She took advantage of it to leave Mrs. Mayor, and went into the living room. Just inside the door, she stopped.

It was as if she had come up against an invisible wall, a barrier of stone, but one she couldn't see.

Ian stood before the fireplace, hands gripped into a single fist behind his back, his red-gold head bent, as if he were studying the empty hearth. He had, presumably in her honor, put on a pale blue silk jacket. Though beautifully cut, it strained across the breadth of his wide shoulders.

He turned then, turned very slowly, and stood still, looking at Jan.

A shaft of sun, cutting through the huge window,

31

burned in his carefully waved hair, yet his craggy face seemed in shadow.

He waited, hard as the ridges of Mercer Mountain, immobile as the ridges of Mercer Mountain, for what could only have been a brief moment, yet to her seemed endless.

In that brief moment she was conscious of the force in him, the ruthless power.

His deep-set eyes, hot as blue flame, seemed to sear her from under his thick reddish brows.

And yet, when he came forward to meet her, smiling at last, he said, "Miss Olney, I'm sorry for such a poor beginning. I would have had it otherwise, believe me. Poor Ellen was so looking forward to your visit, and so happy about it. But when she saw you, it reminded her, and . . ." He shrugged. "Well, I would have wanted it to be otherwise of course. For all our sakes."

Unable to move, listening to Ian's casual apology, Jan was swept by a sense of deep and profound fear. Something inside her whispered, *Danger, danger.*

She reminded herself that she was Jan Olney. She was twenty-three years old. She was a big girl, and could take care of herself. She always had and she always would. Thinking that, she could hear her father's voice, saying, "You're Jan Olney. You're twelve years old. You're a big girl. You can take care of yourself. You always have and you always will."

There, put into words, was the beginnings of that self-sufficiency which Bill Edwards seemed to dislike, and comforted, Jan found that she could move. The invisible wall had melted away. She felt as if she were drawn toward Ian on gossamer strings, and even as she went to meet him, she changed the thought of gossamer strings to spider's web.

He took her hand in his.

She was suddenly too conscious of her smallness, her femininity.

He stood that way, towering over her, pressing her fingers, for another prolonged moment.

She wondered if he were aware of the aura of force

around him; if he were attempting, deliberately, to make her aware of it, too.

She thought, as he led her protectively to a chair, that his carefully brushed red-gold waves were a sign of vanity. The self-imposed immobility of body and expression had a purpose. He knew that he looked like some great golden god out of an ancient myth. He used that spectacular, almost unnerving surface, to conceal what lay beneath.

But what did lie beneath? Jan wondered.

Having seated her, he went on with his apology. "Yes, I had hoped you would have a calmer welcome. I even thought your coming here would help Ellen." He smiled ruefully. "I suppose that was wishful thinking."

"Will she be all right now?"

"In a few minutes, she'll be sleeping. It's her only relief."

Mrs. Mayor, for once silent, brought in a silver urn, and departed.

Ian bent over a stretched-leather Mexican table, and poured coffee into fine China cups.

It was then, for the first time since she had entered the room, that Jan became aware of Bill Edwards.

He sat in a big chair opposite her. His dark head was black, his dark eyes fixed on her face in an openly speculative look.

She realized that he had been watching her since she first froze at the threshold. She gave him an uneasy smile.

"Get settled down?" he asked.

She nodded.

"You must be tired."

"Not really."

"You're traveling on nerve. You'll feel it after a while."

Ian moved between them, handed Jan a sugared and creamed cup of coffee.

She thought that it was a clue to the man himself. He hadn't asked what she would prefer. He simply decided for her. And decided wrongly. She was too polite to indicate her distaste for sugar and cream. She sipped the coffee once, then set it on the table at her side.

Ian had returned to stand before the fireplace, his hair aglow, his face in shadow, once more.

"I don't know," he said, "just how much David told you about us. About our family."

It was obvious to Jan that he expected no answer. She waited silently.

"It's almost . . . almost as if there were a curse upon us. As if the Ballantines had been marked by fate for every possible agony man can know."

Jan thought that was presuming an importance in the scheme of things that no man ought dare presume.

She glanced sideways from Ian's face to look at Bill, who was listening just as soberly as Ian spoke. And yet she knew, and wondered how she did know, that Bill's turned down mouth was concealing an urge for laughter.

Ian was saying, "My father was a man much like yours, Jan."

She noticed that Ian had dropped the formal 'Miss Olney' without asking her permission. But of course, he had to. They were in-laws, and she was a guest in his house. How long could he go on calling her 'Miss Olney'? She nodded, smiled faintly in acknowledgment.

"Very much like Steven Olney," Ian said. "A doer, a liver, a builder. He made and lost two fortunes, and made a third as well. Oil, you know. Surely you've heard of Ballantine Wells."

Jan hadn't heard of Ballantine Wells. But she didn't consider that surprising. She knew only part of the oil business which concerned her own substantial holdings. But she made a mental note to herself. She had friends who could tell her in a moment anything she had to know about oil wells by any name, anywhere in the world.

"He died ten years ago," Ian went on. "It was as if the rock to which we had all clung simply melted away from us, leaving us floating. I had to take over." Ian's blue flame eyes flashed at Jan. "You must know what that means. I understand you had to face the same responsibility yourself."

She nodded.

"So I am sympathetic to your caution," he went on

smoothly, "to your concern that everything be done absolutely right. I want you to realize that, Jan. I want you to know that I, and Ellen, appreciate your coming here, and your motives for it. Ellen's inheritance, whatever David left her, must be handled properly of course."

Jan said quickly, "That was only one reason for my coming, Ian."

His blue flame eyes fastened questioningly on her face.

She didn't turn to look, but she sensed that Bill had suddenly straightened up.

There was quick, burning tension in the big bright room. She felt it float there for a moment before she smiled gently, said, "Ian, do you realize? I am quite alone in the world. Now that David is gone . . ." She moved her slim shoulders. "There's only Ellen. She *is* my sister-in-law. She loved David. That's why I came to Ballantine Lodge."

The quick, burning tension faded with her words.

Bill rose, moved to the Mexican table, and busied himself there for a moment. Then, passing by Jan, he unobtrusively put a cup of black coffee beside her, and removed the cup she had barely touched.

She smiled her thanks.

"It's good of you to feel like that, Jan," Ian was saying, plainly oblivious of Bill's small attention to her. "Some might resent . . . some might not understand." He paused. When he went on, his deep voice was even deeper, edged with harshness. "It wasn't an easy thing for me to do. To call Ellen home so soon after her marriage. Believe me, Jan. I weighed the decision carefully, and for a long time, before I saw that I had no choice. Thalia . . ." His massive shoulders moved in a regretful shrug. ". . . It seemed then the only way to save her."

"But what happened, Ian? David never mentioned that she was ill."

"She wasn't. Not in those beautiful days in Rome."

"Then . . .?"

"To explain it, I have to go back to when my father died. It had a terrible impact on the girls, on all of us.

I had to take over." Ian paused as if marshalling his thoughts, but when he went on, he asked, "Tell me, Jan, how is it that you, instead of your brother, handled all *your* father's affairs? David is . . . was . . . the older, and a man. It seemed an odd disposition to me. When he told me, I must be honest, it raised some serious questions in my mind. I wondered if Ellen should . . ."

Jan said evenly, "David had his career. It took him all over the world, and it took all of his time and interest. My father knew I was competent, and he trusted me."

Ian's craggy face suddenly softened in a wide grin. "And now that I see you, know you, I understand." He moved toward the door, an abrupt turnabout in mood as well as conversation. "And now, Jan, breakfast. You must think me a dreadful host."

She followed him to the terrace, thinking, not that he was a dreadful host, but that he had managed, quite gracefully, to leave her original question about Thalia unanswered.

Thalia had not been ill in Rome.

Something had happened after the Ballantines returned home. Thalia had needed Ellen, so Ian had sent for her. And . . . ?

The wrought-iron table was covered with snowy linen, china that sparkled in the sunlight, silver that gleamed.

"I was just about to call you," Mrs. Mayor cried, hovering plumply nearby. "Now you must sit down, and eat and rest. Now you must enjoy the lovely view."

Bill held Jan's chair for her, then sat next to her.

Ian sat alone across from them.

Mrs. Mayor served waffles and slices of succulent ham, and mounds of eggs, and more steaming coffee, quick conversation pouring like sweet syrup over the silent three. When she had finally withdrawn, leaving them enwrapped in their private cloaks of stillness, Jan tried to think of some way to draw Ian back to talking about Thalia.

But he, methodically eating, his blue flame eyes surveying the terrace, the view beyond, in quick brooding glances, seemed to have completely forgotten Jan's presence.

It was Bill who said finally, "Ian, you don't suppose, do you, that Ellen's marriage to David could have led to Thalia's illness?"

Ian's face hardened. "How could I have known? I wanted Ellen to be happy. I wanted her out of this house." He turned to Jan. "Can you understand that?"

Wondering, Jan said, "I think so, Ian."

"So much had happened, you see. First my father died. Then four years ago, my mother had a terrible stroke. It . . ." He paused. His blue flame eyes shifted upward to a window above the terrace. "It did everything but destroy her completely. And for Thalia, Ellen . . . young Carl . . . Four years ago they were children, you see. It was such an awful blow after the loss of our father. It was so hard to live with. Then about two years ago, Thalia fell in love." Ian swallowed noticeably. "It should have been good but, it wasn't. She chose a . . ." Ian shrugged. "There's no way to say it except straight out. She chose a fortune hunter. She was young, lovely, and could have had any man she wanted, but . . . well, I couldn't allow it. I'm ashamed to say that I bought him off. It was the only way. Thalia was heartbroken. There seemed to be only one thing to do. I took Carl out of school, and Thalia and Ellen, and we traveled. I thought the answer was to take them away, to help them all forget the sorrow that fate seemed to have thrust on Ballantine Lodge. And then, Ellen met David, and fell in love." Ian shrugged. "How could I refuse her happiness? So I permitted, I even encouraged, the quick marriage to David." He sighed heavily. "If I had known . . ." His blue flame eyes came up to meet Jan's gray gaze. He added simply, "But I believe in love at first sight, you see. I believe in love."

She felt the impact of that deep hard force in him. She sensed the compelling quality which made him seem to move everyone around him as if they were will-drained pawns, playing a game in which only he knew the rules.

He went on slowly, the harsh edge in his deep

voice rasping, as if he had to force the words out. "So we left Ellen, radiant in her joy, with David, and we started back for New York. I had planned to stop to see you then, Jan. We had promised David that we would. But I had word that my mother had taken a bad turn. We rushed here. It was a confused time. I didn't even try to phone you. And just when things calmed down, the Ballantine curse struck again. Thalia collapsed. We tried everything. Everything, Jan. And at last, much as I dreaded to do it, I had to send for Ellen. They had always been so close, in age, in heart, in mind. I thought only Ellen could save Thalia. But then, when Thalia . . . when she died, poor Ellen . . ." He stopped. His blue flame eyes flickered at Jan. "You know the rest. You've seen how Ellen is."

There was a moment of silence.

Somehow the hot sun seemed to have moved away. A chill shadow hung over the terrace.

It was all so plausible. One tragedy following another, effects spreading, until David had died alone, with Ellen's name on his lips. Jan winced at that thought.

But she said softly, "I'm sorry. I hope I can help Ellen."

The words were barely past Jan's lips when some sound, a muted cry, an anguished wail quickly stilled brought Ian to his feet.

"I must go in," he said. "Bill, look after Jan for me, will you?"

Jan got up. "Perhaps, Ian, if I go with you . . . perhaps, I . . ."

He shook his red-gold head. "No, you'll see her of course. But later, later. When she's calm again. You'll see and talk with Ellen. And I want you to meet my mother, too. You mustn't think we're uncivilized, Jan. We want you to enjoy your brief stay with us. We want you to know that you're welcome. But now . . ." He paused, raised his head as if listening, waiting for a repetition of that muted sound.

Jan heard nothing more, but he, smiling at her quickly, swung away, and hurried into the house.

She turned to look at Bill.

His dark head was raised. He had that poised, hunter look on his face.

"Ellen?" she asked.

He didn't answer.

Jan shivered, and just then, there was a brief single wail that went quickly still.

Chapter 5

"IT'S ALL RIGHT," Bill said quickly, reassuringly, his dark eyes full of sudden awareness. "Ian will be able to handle it."

"Then it is Ellen?" Jan asked.

"Of course. Who else could it be? Old Mrs. Ballantine is mute, deaf, quite paralyzed."

Jan shuddered, closed her gray eyes.

"You can see now what Ian means by the Ballantine curse."

She said evenly, "I'm afraid that I don't believe in curses. What you mean is that they've had an extraordinary amount of bad luck."

Bill grinned. "You're a cool one, aren't you?"

"I?"

"I saw your face while he was telling you about it. I saw your face when you heard her cry out. You registered everything right. Sympathy, distress . . . yes, of course, everything. And now . . ."

"I feel sympathy, Bill."

"I know you do. But now, your curly little head is hard at work, isn't it? You're fitting together what he told you, taking pieces and making whole out of them."

"Am I?"

His grin faded. He said soberly, "And that is just what you mustn't do. Even though you feel that David suffered, needing Ellen before he died, even though you believe Ian should have sent her to David, remember that what happened was in the nature of the situation. It couldn't be helped. Truly. Leave the Ballantines and their curses to Ballantine Lodge, Jan. Get whatever you have to get done here, and then get out."

"Oh, I will," she promised, asking herself why he was so anxious to see her gone.

Ever since they had driven away from the tiny train station in Mercer, he had insistently told her, in one way or another, that nothing was wrong in Ballantine Lodge. Was it because he knew what she only suspected? That something *was* wrong?

It seemed to her then, sitting in the no longer hot sunlight, that it shouldn't take very long to discover the truth.

Why doesn't Ellen come? David had cried.

What's happened to her?

What do her letters mean?

Jan's throat felt swollen with held-back sobs.

She had already learned some of the answers.

She must see Ellen, talk to her, to learn the rest of them.

Bill was saying, "The money, that in itself, can't really mean anything to you, Jan."

"The money?" she asked blankly.

"What Ellen inherits . . ."

But Jan was thinking that it had all begun somehow with Thalia. "Bill, how did Thalia die?" she asked abruptly.

He pushed back his chair, got up and went to stand at the edge of the terrace.

Jan said, "Bill?"

He swung around. "I told you. Get your business attended to, and get out of here."

"And you?" she asked sweetly, smiling so that her cheeks dimpled. "How long do you plan to stay on?"

"I don't know."

"Then . . . ?"

"That doesn't concern you." A frown gouged lines between his dark brows. Brackets appeared at his long mouth. "Jan, did David ever tell you that some of the Ballantines, Ian at least, possibly the others, had known your father somewhere years ago?"

"Why, no."

"And he never mentioned Ballantine Wells?"

"Never. He was so ill. There was so little time. He

thought of nothing but Ellen." Jan faltered to a stop.

The hard lines faded from Bill's face. He came back to the table. "Here. Have some more coffee." He poured for both of them, sat down next to her.

She didn't want any more, but remained there, hoping that Ian would soon return.

Bill caught her looking toward the doorway.

He grinned. "That's a lot of man, isn't it?"

"I suppose so."

But she was wondering what lay behind Bill's dark eyes. Eyes that never smiled. Even when he grinned.

They were both quiet for a moment.

Then she asked, "Why won't you tell me about Thalia?"

He gave Jan a quick, impatient look. Then, "All right. But listen, Jan, I'm sure it's something Ian would just as soon you didn't know. So . . ."

"I understand."

"I'll tell you only to keep you from asking him."

She waited.

"Thalia . . ." Bill took a deep explosive breath, then reached out and caught Jan's hand. "Thalia fell from here, Jan."

"Fell? From here?" Jan gasped.

His fingers tightened around hers. She clung to the strength he offered, clung to his strength, and even then, in the midst of shock, she was aware of something more than strength in his touch, aware of a sweet hot electricity that seemed to flow between them.

"Do you mean . . . Do you mean she died, like that, in an accident, when Ellen was here?"

"It's listed as an accident in the records," Bill told Jan matter-of-factly. "I went and looked. So I know."

"But if it were an accident . . . if she simply . . ." Jan stopped. "No, Bill. I don't understand. If Thalia wasn't sick, but actually died accidentally, then why did Ian send for Ellen? Why didn't Ellen go back to David? Why . . . ?"

"It's *listed* as an accident," Bill answered, faintly stressing that one word.

"You're implying that she committed suicide, aren't you, Bill?"

He didn't answer her.

Jan sat motionless, her hand still clutching his, her fingers numb with pressure.

Thalia had had a breakdown, and Ian had sent for Ellen, hoping that Ellen could help her sister. But while Ellen was home, Thalia committed suicide. And then Ellen herself had broken down.

Jan shivered.

Ian had said that the Ballantine family was cursed. It was true. True.

And the letters Ellen had written? Those pleading, frantic letters that begged for help, for rescue? Had they been written after Thalia's death? Had Ellen's terror been a product of a mind disordered by the loss of her sister?

Had Ellen been happy that Jan was coming, and then, burdened by guilt at her desertion of David, broken down at Jan's arrival?

And Bill?

Could Jan believe him?

Did he, like she herself, have some private reason beyond the one given, for lingering at Ballantine Lodge?

She drew her hand out of his, the sweet electricity fading as her fingers were reluctantly freed.

A wave of heat swept into her cheeks, for Ian, suddenly towering over her, said, "Finished breakfast, have you?" his blue flame eyes glowing with amusement, and with what appeared to be brotherly approval.

She didn't answer him.

But Bill, laughing softly, got up, excused himself, and went into the house.

Ian took the white leatherette seat across from hers. "I'm glad you waited for me, Jan."

"I thought we might talk some more."

"We have to." He sighed. "Well, you've seen Ellen. So you know how it is now. She was just beginning to recover, you know, when we heard of David's illness."

"So I understand," Jan said.

"I told you before. I'm sorry I brought Ellen home.

But that's over with and done now. When we heard about David, I had to decide what to do. I didn't want to frighten him, to burden him, so . . ." Ian shrugged. "It seemed the only way."

"He was waiting for a plane reservation to come here," Jan said. "And he fell ill . . ."

"If only I . . ." Ian sighed. Then, "When you called, there was nothing I could do. I had to let Ellen talk to you. She collapsed again immediately, and has been in and out of hysteria ever since."

"What have you done for her, Ian?"

"Done?"

"Doctors . . . There's so much nowadays. Perhaps she should be in a hospital. Perhaps . . ."

Ian's craggy face hardened. "Are you telling me that you want me to label her as mad? Do you want me to ruin her life forever?"

"I want you to save her life."

"You don't understand." Ian's deep voice rasped out. "Ellen will be all right. She just needs time." He paused. Then went on more gently, "Just as you need time. Believe me, Jan, I haven't forgotten that you too, have suffered a loss, a bitter loss that has left you all alone."

She winced, thinking of David, as Ian, she knew, had intended she should.

"You must consider us family, Jan."

She looked steadily into his blue flame eyes. "Thank you, Ian."

He seemed about to say something more, but then Mrs. Mayor bounced out of the house. "And have you enjoyed your breakfast, dear Jan? Will you have a nap now? Oh, I know, you young people never do feel tired, do you? but still, it does catch up with you. A good sweet nap, and then a walk in our lovely cedars. And then . . ."

Ian smiled at Jan. "Shall we go in?"

They left Mrs. Mayor still twittering.

In the foyer, Ian said, "I hardly know how to treat a guest, Jan. I'm afraid this house . . ."

"I'm not a guest. I'm one of the family, as you so kindly told me a little while ago."

He nodded an acknowledgment. "This house is no place for the young, nor for the bereaved, I'm afraid."

Jan instantly wondered if that were a hint. If he, like Bill, but in a more oblique fashion, were telling her that she wasn't, in fact, wanted in Ballantine Lodge.

She said, "It's better for me to be here, with you and Ellen, at a time like this, than to be alone, Ian."

Again he nodded an acknowledgment. "There's a dearth of entertainment here, I'm afraid. Perhaps, with Bill, you'll find some diversion."

"I'd rather rest, and think, than be diverted."

Ian smiled, touched her cheek. "You're so like David, aren't you?"

It was a curiously gentle gesture, yet she had to force herself to accept the touch. She had to force herself to return the smile.

"I suppose we are alike," she said at last.

"Forgive me if I leave you now, Jan. You do understand? There is a great deal for me to do always."

"Of course. I thought I would go up to my room for a while. But Ian, when may I . . ."

He was already turning away. He swung back. "What, Jan?"

"When will I see Ellen again, Ian? And when can I meet your mother?"

He frowned, the reddish brows drawing together in a heavy line. "You realize what happened when you arrived, Jan. Ellen . . ." He shrugged. "Well, perhaps by tonight . . . we'll just have to see, won't we?"

"I'll take all the time necessary, Ian. I don't want to hurt Ellen. Only to help her."

"And as for my mother, poor soul. We must wait for a good day. She does have them occasionally." His blue flame eyes shot a glance up the stairs. "Yes, I'm sure we'll be able to manage that quite soon."

The usual absolute certainty was in his voice, but Jan, as she went up to the second floor, felt his glance follow her, and wondered if she imagined some small reservation in his words, some almost physical withdrawal in his reply.

The upper hallway was empty, but she heard a sweet, light voice saying, "There we are, all comfy now? Oh, you do seem to understand. I wish I knew what to say to you. Oh, dear . . . what's the matter now?"

The door at the end of the corridor was half open, showing a narrow wedge of shadowy room.

Jan stared at it. It was from there, from that dim room that she had thought herself watched earlier, to that room an eavesdropper had retreated.

She waited. A figure of white passed the half open door, paused to peer at her. Then there was a muffled exclamation, and the door swung shut, briskly, finally, shut.

But Jan had seen enough.

The figure in white was a nurse.

The room must be the one in which Mrs. Ballantine stayed.

Had it been from there that Jan had heard the dulled muted wail?

It seemed possible, for from there, too, windows would look down on the terrace.

But then Jan remembered that Bill had told her Mrs. Ballantine was mute, deaf, paralyzed, as a result of a stroke many years before.

Jan hadn't heard Mrs. Ballantine cry out then.

Could it have been Ellen? Jan asked herself.

Bill had said it was . . . And yet . . . ?

Jan went into her room. It was still bright with sunlight, hot with sunlight. But she shivered as odd tremors of fear flickered along her bare arms.

The very silence of the house seemed to whisper to her again, to whisper that she must flee. Flee from madness and suicide. Flee from further madness.

From the curse of the Ballantines.

She went to the blue-draped window.

The sun was high now, leaving the terrace in shadow.

She thought of Thalia, slim and blonde and young, staring down at the same red rock ridges at which Jan now stared. Staring at them, and then flinging herself forward to die upon them.

Poor Ellen had come home, hoping that her love would be the medicine to cure Thalia, but Ellen's efforts had been useless.

How long, Jan wondered, had Ellen struggled with Thalia? When had Thalia died? And when had Ellen written those frantic letters to David? What did they mean?

Jan turned away from the window.

The answers were not to be found on the easterly horizon. The answers lay within the big sprawling wings of Ballantine Lodge.

Chapter 6

SHE DRESSED carefully that evening.

Ellen had worn stark black, the widow's uniform, from which her thin arms hung sickly pale.

But Jan did not believe in mourning. Black would not return David to her, nor to Ellen. It would serve only as a bitter reminder of permanent loss.

Jan chose pale blue, a slim, fitted dress that hugged her body, hoping the color would not offend Ellen's feelings.

It was necessary to gain Ellen's trust, her liking. It was necessary to gain her understanding.

The promise to David must be fulfilled.

She reminded herself of that when she went downstairs, and directed by Mrs. Mayor, she went to the terrace. There, seeing Ian, she froze at the threshold. She froze before the same invisible barrier, the same unwillingness to join him, that she had experienced in the morning.

He stood with his back to her, big hands in a single fist behind him. He was bathed in the raw red light of a reflected sunset. He stood like one of a race of gods, in abandoned defiance.

She watched him, silent, unmoving, until Bill touched her shoulder.

She turned then, feeling half-blinded either by the raw sunset, or the aura around Ian. She turned and looked into Bill's face.

His dark eyes were oddly shuttered, his long, turned-down mouth unsmiling. "You'd do well to eat and run this time, Jan."

She didn't answer.

His hand tightened on her shoulder.

Instantly she felt a sweet electric thrill. She pulled

48

away from him, and saw his dark eyes narrow. She turned on her heel and went on to the terrace.

Ian's eyes swept her from dark shining curls to tiny blue-shod feet in an openly admiringly look. "I'm glad that we have managed somehow to maintain some of the amenities here. Seeing you, seeing how you look, reminds me of what I have missed." The gentle, caressing tone, with which he addressed Jan, went out of his voice as he gestured toward Bill. "Would you?"

"I sure would," Bill retorted, and went to the wrought-iron table, which had been set up as a bar.

Ian took Jan's hand. "You must see the view."

She allowed the pressure of his fingers, his enveloping strength, to draw her with him to the edge of the terrace.

"It changes," he was saying. "Every moment of the day it has a different mood."

She shivered, looking down at the red ridges, the great swirling red shadows of reflected sunset.

She was thinking of Thalia.

But Ian obviously was not.

He went on, the gentle caressing note in his voice once more. "It touches you, doesn't it?"

Jan nodded.

"Mountain and meadow . . . not everyone can appreciate them. It takes a special soul . . ."

Bill broke in. "Ready, Jan? Ian?" and handed them wide crystal goblets.

Ian's blue flame eyes flicked at Jan. "To you, to your stay with us."

"To your health, Jan," Bill added, his dark eyes shuttered, his long mouth turning down with his words.

To her health . . .

That was what Bill had said.

Jan sensed the warning, or was it a threat? behind the casual word.

She managed to answer both men as if she had accepted their toasts at face value.

While they chatted, she tried to picture Ellen dressing, Ellen coming down the stairs, Ellen joining the group on the terrace. But Ellen had still not made an appearance when Mrs. Mayor came out to say, "Dinner is ready now. Oh, do come in, do. It will all be spoiled if you wait. Roast beef, you know. So do come in."

Ian took Jan's arm, led her inside, leaving Bill to follow.

A round table had been set in the corner of the huge living room. There were three placemats on the waxed mahogany, three services.

Jan looked at them, then looked at Ian. "But what about Ellen?"

"I'm sorry, Jan. She sends her apologies. She can not come down tonight."

"Then perhaps, after dinner, I could go up and talk to her."

Ian said smoothly, "She must have her rest, Jan. Surely tomorrow is soon enough." Without waiting for a reply, he drew back Jan's chair, seated her, then began to pour wine.

With that chore done, he sat back, smiling at her. "It is almost as if you had brought a bit of festivity to this sorrowing house."

"Is it?"

"Not that I have forgotten, Jan. Believe me, I haven't. I never will. But . . ." His massive shoulders moved in a heavy shrug. "A man must go on, must live . . ."

"We all must," Jan agreed.

He lifted the wine goblet to his lips. "And this is to you also, Jan. To your stay at Ballantine Lodge."

Bill suddenly grinned. "How long *do* you plan to stay, Jan?"

She slid a sharp gray sideways glance at him, knowing he was trying to get her to commit herself before Ian as she had refused to commit herself to Bill.

Then she grinned, too, gave him the answer that he had earlier not considered satisfactory. "I don't know really. First I want to see what I can do for Ellen." Jan turned to Ian. "Forgive me. I know you've tried, are trying, all that you can. But I owe it to David. I'm sure you understand. And besides that, there is the matter of the documents."

"That," Ian said, "should not take such a great deal of time."

"It's all very complicated indeed," Jan said vaguely. "No doubt you remember that from when you handled the same sort of thing yourself."

"Still . . . merely a matter of form, signatures . . ."

Jan managed to make a smile for him, conscious of the dimples in her heartshaped face, conscious of the false innocence in her gray eyes. But at the same time, she was warily assessing the quality behind his words. She sensed a carefully restrained eagerness in him. An eagerness for what? she asked herself. That the estate be settled quickly? But why? The Ballantines obviously had plenty of money. She stopped herself. She was simply assuming that they had money, assuming that what Ian told her was the truth, assuming that the trappings of wealth meant wealth. How did she know? How could she find out, either confirm or not confirm, what he had said? She had already thought of the answer. Her friends could give her what information she needed. But to write would take too long. And the phone . . . There was a way, only one way, to ensure privacy while she called. She could get Bill to take her into Mercer. Then she would know if Ian were eager to have the estate settled quickly because he needed the money. Or . . . or if he was simply anxious to see her gone from Ballantine Lodge.

Either way, though, she would not leave until she had spoken to Ellen, had heard from Ellen's own lips what her letters to David meant. Until she was certain that her promise, Jan's promise to David had been kept, and she could turn her back on the Ballantines forever.

"Perhaps, by tomorrow," Ian was saying, "Ellen will be calmer. Like my mother, she has her good days and her bad days."

"I hope tomorrow will be a good day," Jan told him sweetly.

His blue flame eyes flashed up at her, then fell away.

Bill broke in with a question about hunting, and managed to completely engage Ian's attention for the rest of the meal.

It was only later, when she had returned to her room, that Jan wondered if Bill had had a reason for interrupting her exchange with Ian at that moment.

Had Bill sensed the question in her mind? Had he feared that Ian, too, would sense it?

It was, she decided, one more thing she must ask Bill. But there were others.

Why had he asked her if David ever told her that Ian had once known their father?

Did Bill know if the Ballantines were as wealthy as they seemed to be?

What did he know about Ballantine Wells?

When did Thalia die?

There were other questions she could ask him, questions about himself, but if he were to answer only those about the Ballantines, she would be content with her beginnings.

If he were to answer only those, and *if* she could believe him, she thought, readying herself for bed.

Something awakened her. Something drew her out of restless sleep, and pulled her up in bed. Something sang along the corridors of her consciousness.

It was moments before she remembered that she had arrived that morning in Ballantine Lodge, moments more before she realized that she had heard, and was still hearing, a faint rustling just beyond her door.

She crept out of bed, threw a robe around her, and went silently to the door. Ear pressed to the panel, she stood there, listening intently.

Yes. Yes, a faint rustle, the whisper of fabric, clothes. Yes. That was a soft sigh. Ellen? Could it be Ellen out there?

Jan eased the door open.

A slim girl in nurse's white gasped, "Oh, I'm sorry,"

and spun away, edging on rubber-soled shoes for the half-open door at the end of the hall.

Jan whispered. "Wait. It's all right. Wait a minute," and recognized the faint rustling sounds that she had heard before.

The young girl's nylon uniform, the rubber-soled shoes. Of course. No mystery there.

She grinned. "You didn't bother me. I just wondered who it was."

"Just me." The young girl nervously patted her sandy hair. "I'm Vera West. I take care of Mrs. Ballantine, you know?" At Jan's nod, Vera went on, "But he won't let me smoke in there. So I come out here sometimes. You won't tell him, will you?"

Jan shook her head.

"Honest, I don't do it often. But sometimes . . . you know? I mean . . . it's a long day and a long night. And he's got so many rules. What a man for rules he is. But she's sound asleep now. She really is. Otherwise I wouldn't take a chance."

"But aren't you afraid he'll hear you?" Jan whispered.

"Oh, he's in the other wing, see that way," Vera pointed past the the staircase. "He can't hear from there. They're clear on the other side. Him, and that Bill Edwards that came the other day."

"Where's Ellen's room?"

Vera shrugged. "She's over there, too. It used to be there." Vera jerked her sandy head at the door across from Jan's. "But now he's got it locked up. And her next to him." Vera took a deep breath. "I thought, when I first came, oh, boy, she'd be company for me, you know? Only . . ."

Jan stared at the door that Vera had said was locked. "I guess she's been too sick."

"Sick in the head." Vera sighed. "I tell you, this is a crazy case to be on for my first one. And that's about all I know. And it's kind of awful, too. I mean . . . being so lonesome." She grinned contritely. "I saw you come this morning. And later on then . . . listen, you won't tell him, will you? I got myself right to your door. I was kind of hoping you'd come out, talk to me . . . Just like I was now, tonight."

Jan laughed. "I guess you really are lonesome."

She thought of her suspicions earlier in the day, the feeling that she'd had that she was being watched. She had been. By lonesome Vera West, who was hoping that the new arrival would be someone to talk to.

Now Vera took a deep drag at her cigarette, looked at the tiny glowing stub, and said sadly, "Well, I guess I better go back in. But you come visit with me, will you? Mrs. Mayor says you're okay. And I can see that for myself. So try and come, will you?"

Jan smiled again at Vera's appealing grin, promised she would visit with Vera, and watched Vera trot down the hall. When the faint glow of light had been closed away from her, Jan turned to the door across the hall.

She tiptoed to it. Holding her breath, she tried the knob.

Vera was right. It was locked, solid.

Jan returned to her room, to her bed, wondering why Ian kept that one door locked, what was behind it, whose room it was.

As she drifted into sleep, she told herself to ignore the small mysteries, to concentrate on the large ones.

To think only of Ellen, of seeing Ellen in the morning.

But at breakfast, Ian made the same excuse he had made the day before.

"I am sorry, Jan. I'm afraid that Ellen still isn't up to seeing you."

"I understand," she said evenly. "Perhaps later."

"Perhaps," he agreed. "And as for my mother . . . well, if you don't mind . . . In a day or two . . ." He paused. Then, "Unless, of course, by then you've completed your business with Ellen and decided you must leave. Not . . ." and his eyes met hers full on, "not that I want you to, or ever will want you to."

There was a broad smile on his craggy face. His red-gold waves were brushed and shining. He wore a fine white broadcloth shirt, open at the throat, and slim-cut tan trousers.

She felt herself freeze before the impact of his delibrate charm.

Bill asked, breaking into an oddly breathless silence, "Want a ride to Mercer, Jan? It would give you a chance to look around."

She agreed, delighted that she hadn't had to ask him to drive her in, as she had planned the night before.

Ian, his smile suddenly gone, said, "You will be back for lunch?"

They promised that they would be.

As they left the room together, Ian asked, "Oh, yes, Bill, I meant to talk to you . . . there's something you could do for me when you go up to Denver."

"Sure, Ian. Anytime." Bill grinned, all easy amiability.

"It depends however, on when you're going to make the trip."

"Oh, pretty soon. Another couple of days, I suppose," Bill told him, and took Jan's arm.

She saw his easy grin fall away.

She saw the hunter look return to his face.

They went outside, on to the terrace, and the laughing Bill who could so easily ignore Ian's rather too-obvious hint was completely gone.

"What's the matter?" she demanded.

But he shook his dark head, and still holding her arm, led her across the terrace in long, free, swinging strides, so that she had to half-run to keep up with him.

"What's the matter?" she repeated, when they had reached the car.

"It's beginning to happen," he said shortly. "You've come, you see, and now it's beginning to happen. The first step is to stall you, until he can get rid of me."

"But what are you talking about, Bill?"

He ignored her question. "But getting rid of me isn't going to be easy." He grinned then. "You ought to know that by now. And listen, Jan, you watch out for him. Or he'll charm you, yes, that's what I said, charm you, don't frown, the way a cat can manage to charm a canary."

She couldn't help herself. In spite of the frightening

words, in spite of his serious voice, she burst into laughter.

"Oh, Bill, I'm not a canary."

He laughed with her. "Forgive me then."

But his laughter died when she asked, the small pleasant moment of closeness forgotten, "Bill, when did Thalia die?"

"What difference does it make?"

"I just want to know."

He swung away from her, started the car. He backed from beside the big black limousine to the dusty road. He maneuvered carefully, turning around.

She said, "If you don't tell me, I'll go and look it up myself, you know."

He swore softly, his long mouth turned down. He kicked the car into reckless speed, leaving long trailing plumes of red dust floating behind them, as he sped toward Mercer.

She waited, as imperturbable before his anger as he had been before Ian's broad unhost-like hints.

Finally, Bill sighed. He told her the hour, the day, the date, of Thalia's death.

Jan felt the color drain from her face.

She didn't have to check. She didn't have to take down the file, to look at Ellen's letters.

They had been written months before Thalia's death. Months before Ellen's breakdown.

"What difference does it make?" Bill demanded, his dark eyes watching Jan.

"I don't know," she said thoughtfully. And added, hoping he would believe her, "Probably none."

Chapter 7

THE MERCER MONSTER, that splintering ter -foot log, studded with nails, and tin, dressed in its metal cap, to be a travesty of a man, sparkled in the middle of the small square.

Bill parked the car across from it.

After one quick glance, Jan averted her eyes.

He grinned at her. "You're sensitive, aren't you?"

"It's so ugly."

"It is. Or what it stands for?"

"Greed. That's what it stands for." She didn't say any more. But she wondered why the debris-studded figure reminded her of Ian. She dismissed that as idle imagination, and asked Bill, "What did you mean when you said that it was beginning. What's beginning, Bill?"

"I'm not sure I know yet. But I will know."

"What do you suspect?"

He didn't answer her.

"Why is Ian trying to get rid of you, but being so discreet about it? Why is he stalling me?"

"Maybe Ian wants to see the last of me because he thinks I'm competition."

"Competition?"

Bill grinned. "For your interest, Jan."

She frowned. "Be serious."

"I am." But he was still grinning. Then, "And I suppose he's stalling you because . . . well, maybe he's trying to get Ellen in shape."

"You manage to make it all sound so plausible."

"But you suspect I've got secrets in my hip pocket."

"I'm sure you have."

Bill opened the car door. "The drug store, and the

57

public telephone, which is what I think you're after, is that way. Shall we?"

"Isn't that what you're after, too?"

"I wanted a little time alone with you," he answered.

"Oh?" she said coolly. "But why?"

"Does there have to be a reason?"

"There doesn't have to be, but there is one."

"Let's say I want to make sure that Ian notices he has competition."

She frowned. "You can stop that, Bill." Then, "Why did you ask me if David had ever written anything about Ian, or the other Ballantines, having known my father?"

"Because I wanted to know."

"Do you have reason to think that's true?"

"It hardly matters now, Jan."

"But you *do* have reason?"

"There's just a possibility. And because there is, I wondered about it."

"What suggests the possibility?"

Bill's face closed. "I've said what I'm going to say, Jan." He swung his long legs to the street. "Come on."

She knew it was no use pressing him, so she, too, got out of the car.

Inside the drug store, he gestured toward the phone booth.

She got a handful of change from the wizened proprietor, and sealed herself inside, watching as Bill ostentatiously sprawled on a tiny, round-backed chair, keeping himself well within her line of vision.

There was a two hour time difference between Mercer and New York, which would make it noon in the East. She hoped, as she dialed code, then number, that she would find her stockbroker friend in. He was, and happy to hear from her. So happy that he wasted precious time in personal chitchat. She finally cut in, "A few questions for you. All right?" and went on, "Do you know anything about Ballantine Wells?"

He chuckled. "Do I? A drip in the barrel, a long time ago. Say no to anybody who wants to sell you, Jan."

"Where was it?"

"South America some place. I can find out if you want to know more. Your father almost got rung into it, but he was smart and stayed out."

A quick pulse of fright began to beat in Jan's throat. "What about the name Ballantine. Does it mean anything to you?"

"Say, wait a minute? Wasn't Ballantine the name of the girl David married? What's going on, Jan?"

"Do you know of the Ballantines?"

"I never thought . . . say, it must be the same guy though. The old man died about ten years ago maybe. He'd made it big, three four times. Nothing on them since. They're living off principal, I suppose. Two girls, the boy. All grown by now, I'm sure."

"There was a younger son, wasn't there?"

"I wouldn't think so. But maybe, if he was a baby . . . well, who knows?"

She thanked him, hung up on his anxious queries. When she left the phone booth, Bill asked, "Well?" She shook her head.

He took her place, closed the door against her, watching, she knew, as she walked away just as ostentatiously as he had moments before.

She asked the proprietor for a soft drink.

He got it for her, then settled on elbows in darned shirt sleeves to peer at her through rimless glasses. "You just passing through?"

"I'm staying at Ballantine Lodge."

"Ballantine Lodge?" he cackled. He beat a wrinkled fist on the counter top. "That what they call it now? Pretty fancy is all I can say. Takes more than a year to change a name. We here in town, in Mercer, we call it the young Mercer place."

"Takes more than a year?" she repeated. "Is that how long the Ballantines have been there? Just a year?"

"Less by some months, unless I miss my memory, and I ain't never done that yet. Less than a year. Yep. I can see them coming in, just as if it was yesterday, too. The pretty blonde girl, and the old woman, and the big man." The proprietor gave Jan a suspicious look. "But what you asking me for? You're staying there, you said. You know all that, don't you?"

She shook her dark curly head. "I've just come myself."

"And going soon, I hope. Ballantine Lodge." The old man cackled. "Bad Luck Lodge, better call it. Since the trouble they had there."

Bill had finished his call. He joined her. They left together.

"Find out what you wanted?" he asked.

She nodded. "And what about you?"

"About what I expected."

"And . . . ?"

"Never mind, Jan."

She got into the car. She was puzzled by what she had learned from her broker friend. It was obvious that the Ballantines might have known her father in South America years before at the time that Ballantine Wells came in and went dry. It was possible that, Ian's father having died, the family was living on returns from investment, or even on the principal left to them. And it was possible that their wealth was actually gone. But, to judge by how they lived, their travels, the house, the car, led to the opposite conclusion.

She was more troubled by what the old man in the store had told her. That the Ballantines had had the lodge for less than a year. And Ian, while not claiming otherwise directly, had certainly led her to believe that Ballantine Lodge was the family home, and had been for years.

"You're very quiet," Bill said. "Is it what you learned on the phone?"

She didn't answer him.

"I wish you would trust me," he told her soberly.

She turned, her wide gray eyes searching his face. At last she said, "I wish *you'd* trust *me*."

"But I do, Jan."

"Then tell me who you really are. Tell me why you're here."

For a moment, she thought he was going to answer

her. She saw the beginnings, she thought, of what she could call confidence touch his dark eyes, soften his mouth. But then she saw the withdrawal, the hardening. She saw the hunter look momentarily, and then saw it fade into an easy wide grin.

"Why, Jan, you know who I am." He dipped his head in a mocking bow. "I'm Bill Edwards. I told you that. On home leave from the Consulate in Beirut. Here only to look after poor Ellen, who, and you must agree with me, surely needs looking after."

"I don't believe you," Jan said bluntly.

His easy grin became laughter. "Old Steven Olney was never noted for his tact. Why should I expect it in his daughter?"

And she said thoughtfully, "You really do know quite a lot about my father, don't you, Bill?"

There were just the three of them at dinner.

Ian had made his casual excuses, explaining, once again, that Ellen was unable to join them.

Jan decided to ask him directly if he had ever known her father. If Ian lied, then that small single fact meant something important. If not . . . then she would see.

She waited for the right moment.

It came when Bill asked Ian something about the hunting of game in South America.

She wondered briefly if Bill had given her that opening on purpose, then she turned, smiling, to Ian. "You know," she said, "my father spent a great deal of time there. His business ventures. Did you ever run into him?"

Ian hesitated, his blue flame eyes on her face. Then, "Why, yes, I did. And my father, too. It was, oh . . . let's see . . . more than ten years ago surely. We stayed at the same hotel for a night or two, passed a few hours together. We nearly had a deal on Ballantine Wells as a matter of fact. I'm surprised that Ellen never mentioned it to David." Ian paused. "Or perhaps she did?"

Jan answered, "I'm not sure. David said something . . . but he was so ill . . . it wasn't clear. I might have misunderstood."

When dinner was finished, Ian led Jan out to the terrace.

Bill, uninvited, followed them, perched silently on the stone wall, his face in the shadows.

It was so obvious that Bill was playing watchdog that Jan wanted to laugh, and soon, simply to free him from his self-assigned tasks, she excused herself and went up to her room.

It was very early. A pale moon silvered the eastern horizon. She paused to admire it, but then, yawning, tired and confused, she decided to go to bed.

Huddled under the light sheet, she thought of the two days just past.

She had come to Ballantine Lodge with questions. In the two days since her arrival, she had received no answers. But the questions had multiplied.

David had cried out of his final fever, *What's happening to Ellen? Why doesn't she come? What do her letters mean?*

Jan had believed that the excuse given, that Ellen was ill, had been no more than that, an excuse for desertion.

Now Jan knew that Ellen had had a breakdown.

The results of it were real, tangible.

And that was why she couldn't go to David when he needed her.

But the letters had been written to David before Thalia died, before Ellen herself became ill.

Why had Ellen written those letters then?

What had she feared in Ballantine Lodge?

Was there some connection Jan couldn't see between Ellen's pleas for help, and Thalia's suicide?

Jan twisted and turned uncomfortably on the soft mattress. She closed her eyes against the shadows that seemed to creep through the room.

Ian had acted horrified at her suggestion that he should provide professional care for Ellen.

He wanted the business of Ellen's inheritance settled, yet he obviously was not anxious that Jan spend any time with Ellen.

He had given Jan the idea that the Ballantines had

always lived in the lodge on Mercer Mountain, yet he and his mother and Thalia had come there barely a year before.

The suspicion, sharpened by intuition, was a certainty now.

There was something terribly wrong in Ballantine Lodge.

She had sensed it first in the whispering silence. Now, beneath the shadowy patina of unanswered questions, she saw a faint pattern emerging.

She pictured Ian as she had first seen him, hard as the ridges of Mercer Mountain, immobile as the ridges of Mercer Mountain, the sun turning him into a great golden god, the aura of force, power, surrounding him.

She shivered, and drew the sheet more closely around her, and through the rustle of movement, she heard a faint click.

Instantly, she sat up.

She listened.

She thought it might be Vera, smoking a cigarette in the hall, hoping for a chat in the middle of the night.

Jan pulled on her robe, went out.

In the pale glow of the dim night lamp, she saw that Mrs. Ballantine's door was closed.

The faint click had not been made by Vera West.

Jan looked at the door across from hers. The door that Vera had said was locked, now that Ellen no longer used her old room.

It had been locked the night before when Jan tried it. But now, as she listened to the whispering silence, she crossed to it, tried it again. It swung open.

The room was full of pale moonlight.

It wove silver threads on the shadowed walls, silver veils on the white coverlet, a silver halo around Ellen's head.

Jan gasped, nearly cried out.

For one wild, terror-stricken moment, she thought that Ellen must be dead.

She lay curled on the pillow, a small hand at her lips, her body as slight as a child's. Her glowing hair fell in a shining curtain across her shoulder. And then, as if sensing eyes that watched her, she stirred and sighed.

Jan held her breath, drew back softly.

She wished that she could awaken Ellen, speak to her then. But Jan was reluctant to disturb the rest that Ellen so obviously needed.

It would have to wait, Jan told herself. There would be other opportunities. If not, she would have to make them.

As she closed the door, she heard the faint click again, the same sound that she had heard from within her room.

Ellen must have gone into the moonlit room, flung herself on the bed and immediately fallen into a deep sleep of terrible exhaustion, so that when Jan found her moments later she was completely unconscious.

Jan, turning to her own door, thought such a sleep was a symptom of illness.

As she touched the door knob, a huge shadow seemed to lunge at her.

She cringed against the wall, with the shadow enveloping her, drowning her, unable to move, to cry out.

And then the shadow became Ian. Big, immobile Ian, who said softly, "That was Thalia's room, you see. Poor Ellen was so close to her in life. Now she goes to Thalia's room to be close to her in death. I can not allow that. Of course you understand."

Jan nodded, too numb to speak.

Frightened, yet not knowing why, sensing a threat in Ian that she couldn't name, she waited.

He watched her for a moment, his blue flame eyes searching her face.

Then he smiled. "I must go in now. I'll take Ellen back to her own bed. And then I'd better find the key. I can not allow her to torment herself this way. I must find the key she used to unlock the door to Thalia's room."

Chapter 8

IN THE MORNING, there was a new brass lock on the door across the hall from Jan's.

So she knew that it no longer mattered if Ian had found the key, or how Ellen had gotten it. She would no longer be able to slip into Thalia's room. Ian had seen to that.

His reasons seemed plausible enough, yet Jan, uncomfortably remembering how his shadow had lunged at her, enveloped her, the night before, wondered if they were the true reasons.

She gave the new brass lock a thoughtful look before she went downstairs.

Ian and Bill were in the living room.

She could hear the counterpoint of the two deep voices.

She paused in the foyer, listening.

She wore a sleeveless cotton dress in pale green, small flat shoes in exactly the same shade. Her dark shining curls were brushed back, emphasizing her wide gray eyes, eyes touched now with the pale green of her dress.

The two men were talking about South America again. Bill seemed inordinately interested in that area.

She wondered if he had ever been there. She wondered where he was born, where he had gone to school. She wished that she knew everything about him.

Everything, instead of the nothing that she actually knew.

The two deep voices made a counterpoint. Listening, Jan didn't want to go in, interrupt. She didn't want to face Bill's unsmiling dark eyes, nor Ian's blue flame look.

She reminded herself that she was Jan Olney, a big

girl. She could take care of herself. She always had and always would. It was as if her father was speaking to her.

She straightened her small shoulders, set her lips in a curved smile, consciously deepened her dimples, and crossed the threshold, saying, "Good morning," in a bright cheerful voice.

The deep counterpoint of voices stopped. The unsmiling dark eyes regarded her with obvious disapproval. The blue flame eyes stared at her with obvious admiration.

Bill, disapproving . . . she knew why. She was interfering with him in some way that she didn't understand.

Ian, admiring . . . she dared not accept the surface explanation. Then why?

They had breakfast together.

Afterwards, Ian apologized, saying he had things to attend to, and left Bill and Jan alone.

Bill raised his dark brows. "What are you going to do? This can go on forever. And you have to see Ellen sometime."

"I can wait," Jan told him evenly.

"It may take longer than you think."

She shrugged, hoping the careless gesture covered her deep sense of the wrongness in Ballantine Lodge.

Wait is what she did.

The long slow hours of the next two days seemed to multiply endlessly, to multiply as her questions, and yes, as her fears multiplied.

Ian intimated more than once that he would be glad to take the documents to Ellen, to have her sign them, but Jan, determined to talk to Ellen, to find out what her letters had meant, managed to act as if she had not understood Ian's hints, and he, for his own reasons, didn't do more than intimate.

Bill trailed her, an easy smiling presence. Yet, behind his grin, she sensed a wariness. He was watching her, just as she was watching him.

Then, unexpectedly, just as she had begun to believe

that they would go on forever, the long slow hours came
to an end.

She awakened with hot sun on her face that morning,
lay still, and listened to the whispering silence until she
could bear it no longer.

She rose and dressed, determined to escape the house
for a little while. To escape her questions, and yes, she
admitted it to herself, to escape her fear.

Perhaps, out of doors, under the wide arch of the blue
sky, she would find a temporary peace.

She had hoped to go out alone, unseen, but when she
stepped into the hallway, Mrs. Mayor was coming up the
stairs.

Balancing trays on extended fat arms, her wrinkled
round face wreathed in smiles, she beamed, "Oh, there
you are, Jan. Such a fine day, and you up bright and
early. And you should see her this morning. Her dear
old eyes just full of life. It's hard to believe it's true. Why,
only yesterday, poor Mrs. Ballantine was that dull. Like
a stick, a log. And now . . ."

"That's wonderful," Jan said.

"Indeed it is. Although it means nothing. Nothing at
all. Although, I must say, I do like to look on the bright
side. Why not? Still, poor dear. I've seen her that way
before. You'd almost think she could speak, could understand. And then, why . . . overnight . . . It's been that way
in the two months I've been here. Up and down . . . and
hope, and then . . ."

"Two months?" Jan demanded. "Why, I was sure
you'd worked for the Ballantines longer than that."

"Did you, dear? Why no. Just two months. Vera West
and I started about the same time. A week or so apart, I
would think. And that poor child . . . this is no job for her.
A practical nurse on her first case, and young as a morning dandelion, and what's there for her to do? Why, nothing. Nothing. On her time off, that is. What time she gets,
I should say. And when she is working . . . why, it isn't
easy. Believe me, old Mrs. Ballantine, tiny as she is just
isn't easy. As you'll see. You'll see. No wonder Sarah

Jarvis had to give up. She was just too old and tired herself, I guess. She couldn't manage any more."

"Did you know her?" Jan asked quickly.

"I? Oh, my no. She was gone before I came."

The tray tilted precariously on Mrs. Mayor's extended arms.

"Let me help you," Jan offered, hoping for an opportunity to at least see Mrs. Ballantine for a moment.

But Mrs. Mayor shook her head. "Oh, no, dear, I can manage. You go down, do. And have some coffee. It's ready in the living room as every day. And . . ."

Jan thanked her, waited until, with words still trailing her, she knocked at the door of Mrs. Ballantine's room and was admitted by Vera, who grinned and waved, then, with Mrs. Mayor inside, closed the door firmly.

Another of Ian's decrees, Jan thought.

It was obvious now.

She was not to see Ellen yet, nor was she to see Mrs. Ballantine yet.

Jan hurried through the whispering silence. The bright living room was empty, the terrace, too.

Where was Ian? she wondered.

And what about Bill?

But she didn't stop to think about it. She took advantage of the opportunity she had hoped for, and hurried down the long flight of steps to the parking area. From there, she knew, she could reach the road, and the sheltering cedars, and breathe the untainted air outside of Ballantine Lodge.

When she emerged on the road, she paused to look up at the house. Its huge windows seemed to reflect bits of early sun that gleamed at her like menacing, evil eyes. Its wide redwood wings seemed draped in red shadow, which covered the terrace and the red rocks below where Thalia had died.

Jan shuddered, turned away.

But the shadow of Mercer Mountain seemed to follow her into the cool green stand of cedars. The birds went still in the wake of her footsteps. The wind died as she passed. The silence became the whispering silence of Ballantine Lodge.

Sarah Jarvis had left the house just about two months before. And two months before David had been alive, yearning for the bride he could not reach by phone or cable, torn between his duty and his fear for the girl he loved.

Two months before, Jan had been in New York, thinking ahead to when she would meet her new sister-in-law.

With Ellen so desperately ill, why had Sarah Jarvis left?

Jan stopped. She had gone hardly a mile, but she knew she could go no further. She looked back. Nothing moved but swirls of pink dust kicked up when she had passed. She looked ahead. The road curled away beyond a stand of thrusting red rock.

She wavered, taking small steps in a dance of indecision, and in that moment she saw a long black shadow fall beside the rock, and move around it.

Her thin, involuntary cry seemed terribly loud.

It stirred the birds into song, the wind into movement.

Ian.

His huge shadow.

The aura of power around him.

She did not want to see him, not there, in the vast emptiness of mountain and meadow.

She tried to run, but her feet seemed trapped in quicksand.

The shadow came on around the stand of rock, came black and flat, and fell away.

Bill emerged on the road.

She felt her fright melting.

She was weak, wordless.

Bill came to meet her, his easy grin quite gone.

She took a step back. "You scared me."

"I? I scared you?" Then, "At least you *do* have sense enough to be scared. I was beginning to wonder."

"Why are you following me?" she cried.

They stared at each other, both suddenly hot-eyed, and angry.

Then he put his hands on her shoulders.

She couldn't help herself. There was something in his touch that seemed to send sweet singing messages into her. She let herself lean against him.

And he said roughly, "But you're never scared of the right things, Jan."

She drew away, in command of herself now. "And what are they?"

He ignored that. "If you were, you'd go away from here."

"Why?"

He shrugged, and went ahead of her, plainly certain that she would follow him.

She did, wishing that she had the courage to turn her back on him, to go on alone, but glad that he was with her.

He maintained his grim silence until they had reached the stone steps that led up to the terrace.

There, he paused, said, "Be careful, Jan," and then motioned her to go ahead of him.

When she reached the terrace, Ian was waiting in the doorway.

"You've been for a walk," he said.

She nodded.

His blue flame eyes moved from her to Bill.

"It must have been pleasant on the mountain this morning."

She nodded again.

His big golden head went back. "If I'd known you wanted a walk, I would have been glad to take you. But, of course, you did find company."

"We met on the way," Jan explained, annoyed with herself because she felt that he had demanded an explanation, an excuse, from her.

"You went out alone, you mean?" Ian bent to her, a smile touched the corners of his mouth. "You mustn't do that, Jan. This is a wild wild country. There are so many dangers you can't see, can't even imagine."

"So Bill has just been telling me. Yet it all seems peaceful enough."

"Appearances can be deceiving."

She watched him warily, sensing laughter behind his sober words. It was as if they were engaging in two conversations at once. One spoken. One not spoken, but understood. She found herself shivering. Shivering in the white hot sunlight.

Ian turned away abruptly. "Ellen's inside, waiting. She wants to see you now, Jan."

So the long endless hours were finally at end.

Ellen was huddled in the corner of the big sofa, her head back, her eyes closed.

A shaft of sunlight fell across her face, mercilessly exposing the ravages of grief.

Her long hair lay like molten gold on her narrow shoulders. Her thin hands were clenched in her lap.

The mourning black of her dress was in startling contrast to the pink robe tucked around her.

The room was utterly still.

On the threshold, unable to move, Jan felt trapped in the awful sense of having once before lived through that same moment.

She stood there, slender, vulnerable, her heartshaped face completely blank, her curved lips frozen in a half smile, her silver eyes wide. Memory of the pictures David had sent her drifted through her mind.

Ellen?

Was this thin, haggard girl the Ellen that David had married?

Was this the joyful, laughing Ellen who had hugged David on the Spanish Steps? And looked up at him adoringly at the Coliseum? And . . .

Beside her, Jan could feel Ian's hard, immobile presence. She sensed the power of him, that held all of them, prolonging the moment in which she looked at Ellen.

Then Ellen stirred. Her golden hair shifted on her narrow shoulders. Her white face tipped up. Her blue eyes opened, glistening with held-back tears.

"Jan?" Her soft voice was husky with tears, too. "Oh,

Jan, I'm so sorry it has to be like this. I had such good dreams . . . David and me together. Oh, Jan . . ."

Ellen.

It *had* to be Ellen.

"David . . . how could I have lost him, Jan? What happened? Why did it happen?"

Released at last from the spell of her doubt, Jan went to sit beside Ellen. "We don't know the answers to those questions, Ellen."

"But he was my life. When he died, then nothing mattered any more. Nothing, Nothing."

Ian said quietly, but with an odd note of warning, "Now, Ellen, if you over-excite yourself . . ."

"No, Ian. Please . . . I want to talk to Jan." Ellen's wide eyes went to Ian in a quick pleading look. "I'll be good. I promised, didn't I? I just want to talk to Jan. I want to talk about David. Ian, I *have* to talk about David."

"But remember to be careful," he answered. "You mustn't let yourself get carried away."

Again Jan had the strange feeling that she was listening to two conversations. One spoken. One unspoken, yet understood.

And Ellen cried, "I won't. I promised, didn't I? I'll be calm. I'll be careful. . . ." She stopped, breathless. Then she turned to Jan. "Tell me about him. About David. Tell me everything that I missed. We had so little time. We . . ."

Ian cut in, "Ellen, dear, Jan has other things to discuss with you. You are David's only heir, you know. There are many documents to be signed. There is much business that has to be attended to. Jan's been waiting all this time, and now you . . ."

"Oh, please," Ellen cried. "No . . . no . . . no . . . not now. Please . . . not now."

Jan said quickly, "Of course not, Ellen. It's all right."

Jan didn't want to discuss the settlement of the estate. Not until she had spoken to Ellen alone. Not until she had asked Ellen about the letters written to David. Not until the promise to him had been fulfilled.

But Ian stood there, leaning against the fireplace, his blue flame eyes watching Ellen, watching Jan.

And Bill sat across the room, his dark eyes wary under drawn brows. His dark eyes watching Ellen, too, but with pity, and with . . . with what?

Jan asked herself what she saw in Bill's eyes.

Pity, and . . . ?

Was it love?

She had never, even from the beginning, believed that Bill stayed on because he was concerned about Ellen.

Yet now, seeing him look at Ellen, Jan realized that what he had said might be the simple truth.

Shamed, wondering, Jan asked herself why that thought should hurt, and remembering the sweetness of his touch, she turned away from him.

Ellen, her soft unpainted mouth trembling, whispered, "Jan, do you hate me?"

"Oh, Ellen, no. No. How can you think such a thing," Jan cried. And unwillingly her gray gaze returned to Bill. She saw approval in his dark eyes. Yes. He wanted her to be kind to Ellen. Yes. He . . .

She made herself turn back to Ellen.

It was necessary to tread carefully with Ian watching, listening. Jan knew that, but didn't know how she knew it.

Ellen was sobbing now. "I love David. I would never have let anything hurt him. Not if I could have stopped it."

Ian came, bent over her. "I'm sorry, Ellen. But I think . . ."

"I'll take her to her room," Jan said quickly.

"I think not."

His tone was harsh, plainly warning that nothing Jan could say would change his mind. He wouldn't allow Jan to be alone with Ellen. But why? Why?

Because Ellen, Jan herself, all of them, were pawns in some game Ian was playing, a game in which only he knew the rules.

The faint shadowy pattern . . .

She had sensed it before.

But she said, "If Ellen and I could sit together alone, for a little while, Ian . . . if . . ."

He didn't bother to answer. He drew Ellen to her feet, draped the pink robe around her slim shoulders.

She sagged against him, her head dropping to rest on him. "I'm sorry, Ian. I tried. I did try."

He led her to the foyer.

There, she stopped, hung back. "Listen, Jan, don't go away. Please, please, Jan, don't leave me here."

"I won't," Jan said softly. "I promise you. I won't."

"For David's sake . . ." Ellen's last few words were a pained gasp. Her knees buckled.

Ian lifted her into his arms, and carried her upstairs.

Jan looked at Bill.

"She loved him very much," he said, absolute conviction in his deep voice, yet bewilderment in his eyes.

Jan herself felt the same bewilderment.

Ellen had loved David, and married him, and lost him, but loved him still. And yet . . . ?

Mrs. Mayor bounced in. "My dears, you must be starved. Breakfast is ready on the terrace. Oh, has the poor child gone up again? I did think she was so improved. I did think . . . but then, I am always so optimistic. Think the best, I say. But do come out, do. It's a lovely day. And tomorrow will be lovely, too."

Chapter 9

IT WAS later the same day.

Jan sat on the terrace alone.

Before her the golden meadows sprawled to the empty horizon, pampas grass rippling like wide-touched waves.

Behind her the big house crouched under the red shadow of Mercer Mountain.

She thought that she had made a mistake in not giving the documents to Ellen earlier. But she had been unable to do it, knowing that if she did, Ian would somehow gently and unobtrusively make it impossible for her to see Ellen again, until, just as gently and unobtrusively, he managed to send Jan away from Ballantine Lodge. Once gone from there, Jan knew, she would never know the truth, never keep her promise to David.

She started at a sound, looked up.

Ian smiled at her from the doorway. "You were miles away in your thoughts. Where? In New York? Or in Beirut?"

She kept her face expressionless. Why had he asked if she were thinking of Beirut? she wondered.

"No one can be happy in this house," he went on. "Even you feel that. It's the Ballantine curse, of course."

"You don't believe that, Ian."

"Don't I?"

"But how can you?" she demanded. "Life offers a taste of everything, to everyone. A taste of love, a taste of death."

"A taste of love," he repeated thoughtfully. "A taste of death. How well you put it." He waited a moment. Then, "I would want to see David's sister happy, and forgetting the tragedy that has struck her, and all of us."

"I want to see Ellen happy."

"Ellen?" Ian's blue flame eyes raked Jan's face. "Do you really, my dear Jan? Or . . ." and his deep voice rasped, ". . . do you want to punish her by your presence?"

"Ian!"

"You must realize what seeing you does to poor Ellen. She can hardly bear . . ."

"Ian!" Jan repeated. "I must help Ellen. Don't you see that?"

"Then let her forget."

Jan recognized that this one was a new approach. Another way for Ian to keep Jan from being with Ellen.

She must deal with it directly, she knew. But suddenly she was frightened.

Ian, bending over her, seemed the source of all strength, all power.

She made herself whisper finally, "I'll help Ellen forget, if you let me."

"You? You, who are so like David?" Ian's voice was suddenly soft, caressing. "So very like David. The same straight gray eyes that shift color suddenly. The same dark hair. The same wiry slimness. You're a living reminder. David is dead. But you're a living reminder."

David is dead.

But she, Jan, was alive.

Was there deliberate menace in those words?

She clenched her suddenly shaking hands into small fists. He must not know how frightened she was. She took a long slow breath. Ian must not guess her fear.

She said coolly, "Ian, perhaps we better understand each other. I am not here to hurt Ellen. Nor am I here to deprive her of what is hers, what David left to her. Just in case you suspect that, I want you to know that your suspicions are wrong. The day Ellen is calm enough, well enough, to understand the documents she must sign, to understand what it is my obligation to explain, then I'll see to it that the business is settled as far as I can, and then I'll leave."

His craggy face broke into a warm grin. "Dear Jan, I'm afraid you misunderstand me. *I* don't want you to leave. For my part I would keep you here forever." His huge hand curled around her shoulder, the steel fingers cutting bruises into her shrinking flesh. "Don't you know that, Jan? I would want to keep you with me forever."

And Bill said suddenly, "Is this a private conference, or can anybody join in?"

"Bright as a berry," Mrs. Mayor repeated, as Jan followed her along the hall. "Yes indeed, now's the time to see her. That's why I rushed down to tell Ian. Why, I know you've been waiting, Jan, waiting all this time to meet poor Ellen's mother. And so . . ."

It had been a hard, hot few moments, but Mrs. Mayor didn't seem to realize that.

She had come out to the terrace, her round face aglow. "Why, Ian, your mother's just grand today!"

He'd swung around, almost lunging. "What?"

"Well . . . you know . . . by comparison, I mean." Mrs. Mayor's round blue eyes moved from Ian to Jan. "And so I thought, after she's been sleeping all this time, dozing or whatever, Vera says . . . and today . . . why now's the time for Jan to make her visit, of course."

"It is very difficult for my mother," Ian said quickly. "We don't want to upset her . . ."

"Why, no. No, we don't, do we?" Mrs. Mayor agreed. "But now's the time, I'm sure of it."

Jan was on her feet, smiling prettily at Ian. "Oh, yes, for just a few minutes, Ian. I do so want to meet your mother."

She saw the hesitation in his face and wondered. She asked herself why he was as loathe to have her meet Mrs. Ballantine as he was loathe to allow Jan any time alone with Ellen.

That thought made Jan say insistently, "You know, Ian, it will probably be my only chance."

He said, "Do you understand, Jan? My mother doesn't speak, is completely paralyzed. We can't tell if she hears or not. We don't know exactly how much . . ."

"I understand."

"So that when you say 'meet' her . . ."

"Just to smile at her, Ian. Just to say hello."

He hesitated, then nodded. "But I'll go up first. Just to make sure."

Mrs. Mayor twittered, "But really, believe me . . ."

He gave her a hard blue look and went inside.

"Well, I never," Mrs. Mayor chuckled. "That man . . . you never do know what he's going to do, do you?" She shrugged her plump shoulders. "Like that business about the key. And the new lock on the door." Mrs. Mayor giggled. "You'd think it was Bluebeard's room, wouldn't you?"

Bill and Jan exchanged unsmiling glances.

Mrs. Mayor, insensitive as always, went on, "Oh, it is a funny job. But a job's a job, I always say. I have to keep telling that to poor Vera. She is a strange one, full of all sorts of ideas. But then . . ." Mrs. Mayor beamed, "She's young. Naturally she's full of ideas. Young people always are."

Ian returned, interrupting Mrs. Mayor's friendly chatter. "All right, Jan," he said.

She followed Mrs. Mayor upstairs.

"Bright as a berry," Mrs. Mayor was saying, and paused at the head of the steps. "Not that I want to mislead you, Jan. It's like Ian says. And when I tell you bright as a berry . . . that's just a way of saying she's better."

The door at the end of the hallway stood open.

Vera waited there, sandy head bent forward eagerly, and grinning. "Coming to see us? We sure can stand some company."

"I'm sure you can," Jan said.

Mrs. Mayor beamed. "See, Vera? I told you. As soon as I had seen this one I told you everything was all right. You and your crazy ideas."

"You've got to admit he's peculiar," Vera led the way into the room. "You know what he did just now? Rushed in, said, 'Get out. I want to see my mother.' But what's the matter with him? It's not like he's going to talk to her, tell her secrets that I oughtn't to hear."

For a moment, a sudden roaring seemed to fill Jan's ears. A wave of dizziness washed over her.

The room into which she had followed Vera seemed dark, silent, cool as a tomb.

It was as though fright had sucked all control of her senses away, leaving her a trembling husk.

But then she saw the pale sun through half-open drapes, and she saw the faint yellow of a lamp. And she heard Vera grumble, "Sends me out to stand in the hall, and closes the door, you know? And how about the rest of the time, a couple of times a day, he's in, he's out. I've got to watch her every second he says. He wants to know if she moves. *"If she moves."* Vera's voice was heavy with sarcasm. "Okay. You tell me. How can she move?"

Jan winced. How could Mrs. Ballantine move indeed?

She lay very nearly buried in stacked pillows. Her tiny head, wrapped in thin gray braids, was turned toward the window, so that Jan couldn't see her face. But Jan could see small, bird-like hands enclosed in steel braces, and small, thin legs that made a barely noticeable outtine under the coverlet.

"Sarah Jarvis didn't mind," Vera went on. "That's what he keeps telling me. Oh, you can say what you want, Mrs. Mayor, but there's something wrong with that man. 'Sarah Jarvis did everything for the Ballantines. Always. Sarah Jarvis did everything.' That's what he stands here and says. As if I care about Sarah Jarvis."

"There now," Mrs. Mayor soothed. "It's a good day today, and tomorrow will be better."

"Maybe," Vera retorted, shaking her sandy hair. "If I can make it to tomorrow."

Jan tiptoed around the bed. As she passed the partly open drapes, she threw a shadow on Mrs. Ballantine's face.

The old lady's eyes were closed. Yet Jan thought that she saw a movement, a response, to the quick shadow, from beneath blue-veined and nearly transparent eyelids.

Jan leaned closer. "Mrs. Ballantine? Mrs. Ballantine,

I'm Jan Olney. I'm David's sister. David, Ellen's husband's sister. I've come to visit for a little while."

"There now, dear, do try to understand," Mrs. Mayor said. "She won't hear you, nor answer. She won't follow what you tell her."

Jan nodded. She hadn't expected an answer. She simply felt that she couldn't stand there, stare at the old lady. She had to introduce herself properly, even if she couldn't be heard, responded to.

She drew a chair closer, sat down.

Mrs. Mayor said, "Well, now, I'll go on. And you, Jan dear?"

"In a little while," Jan whispered.

"She doesn't even know you're here," Mrs. Mayor twittered. "But you are a sweet child to care." Mrs. Mayor bounced to the door. "Mind now, you mustn't stay too long," she warned before she went out.

"Ian . . . stand-in for God, I call him." Vera stood across the bed from Jan. "That man . . . Can't smoke in the room. Can't go out for a smoke. Can't hardly live even."

"You can go out now, if you want," Jan suggested. "I'll wait here until you come back."

Vera grinned broadly. "Say, you are nice, you know? I'll be right back."

Jan sighed with relief as Vera hurried out.

She leaned closer to Mrs. Ballantine, whose tiny wrinkled face was the color of old wax.

She put an impulsive hand on the limp, brace-bound arm that lay so still on the coverlet. "Couldn't you try to hear me?"

As she touched the cool flesh, she felt a tiny, involuntary quiver.

There was a flutter of lashes. Transparent eyelids rose. Mrs. Ballantine looked at Jan, surely, the old lady was looking right at her, Jan thought, staring into dazed, tired eyes.

"You did feel my touch, didn't you?" Jan burst out. "You do hear me."

Mrs. Ballantine's hazel eyes were wide with stark terror. With a terror that Jan had seen only once before in her life. She had seen that same look in David's eyes as he lay dying, and whispering of Ellen.

The old lady's eyes suddenly drowned in bright, brimming tears. They slipped along her faded lashes to her crumpled cheeks.

"Oh, please," Jan whispered. "Don't be afraid of me. Please . . . please . . ." She gently wiped the tears away. "Don't be afraid. Just rest now. I'll come back. I'll talk to you again."

As she moved around the bed, she had the feeling that the old lady's eyes followed her.

Vera slipped into the room, closed the door softly. "Close shave. I almost got caught." But she grinned. "He's coming up the steps right now."

"I'll come back soon," Jan promised.

"I wouldn't if I were you. I'm only here because I have to be. Believe me, you hang around with her . . ." Vera jerked her head toward the bed, ". . . and pretty soon you'll think you're going crazy, too."

"What do you mean?"

"Take a couple of days ago. I was getting her ready for her bath, and I had to go in, leave her alone for a minute. Well, I know she can't talk. She can't, not a word, not a sound. And when I'm in the bathroom, getting set up, I heard this sound . . well, okay, so I'm crazy, but I think I heard this sound. So I got out to see, and he, that one, Ian, he comes rushing in here. 'Out,' he told me, and started shoving me to the door as if I was a piece of furniture. So I went out, and I waited, and pretty soon he came and got me. He said she was okay, and sent me in. She sure was okay. She was just like I left her, except she was sleeping again, and that's how she was until this morning. Now, I ask you, how about that? I thought I heard something. Only she couldn't make a sound if her life depended on it."

Jan whispered, "Vera, she might hear you."

"She never has before."

"But you can't tell. That's the thing. You really can't tell."

Vera's face changed. "That's right. You can't," she said thoughtfully. "I mean . . . just because she can't talk and can't move . . ." Vera sighed. "I just don't like this job, you know? And I don't like this house."

Jan returned to Mrs. Ballantine's side.

Her hazel eyes were dry now, still open, but dry, and staring in dazed concentration into Jan's face.

As she watched, Jan saw the concentration fade; thin eyelids fluttered and closed. The old lady sank into sleep.

Jan, back in her own room, listening to the whispering silence, still felt the slight movement of cool flesh under her fingertips, still saw hazel eyes filled with terror.

She had the feeling that Mrs. Ballantine could understand every word said around her, but was paralyzed by terror into permanent silence.

Why had she suddenly wept?

Why did she sleep for days on end?

And why did she suddenly wake?

Why did Ian visit his mother several times a day, and always send Vera out so that he could be alone with her?

Chapter 10

JAN HAD the pictures lined up on the dresser top.

David. Ellen, Thalia, Carl. Ian.

She studied them carefully, looking into each face as if it could tell her what she wanted to know.

She sighed. They told her nothing. Nothing.

And there were so few of them. So few to be the only thing of David's life with Ellen.

She went over them again.

David . . . his dark smiling eyes.

She could hear his feverish whisper, *What's happening to Ellen, Jan? Why doesn't she come? What do her letters mean?*

Ellen had married David, knowing that he could not leave his post until his tour there was done, yet she had left him to return home, then written to beg him to join her.

And there was Ellen . . . long golden hair, slim, dimpled, looking at David with love.

One of Thalia . . . a bit older than Ellen, slim, too, and golden-haired, but hers was cut short, and her eyes were shadowed, somehow withdrawn.

The two girls together, arms linked . . . Ellen looking into the camera. It must have been David taking the picture, for Ellen was looking into the camera with love. Thalia was turned slightly away.

Ian and Carl . . .

Jan wished there was one of Sarah Jarvis.

David had written warmly of the housekeeper, companion, friend, who had raised the girls.

All of them, but Sarah, and in all of them, the ancient backgrounds of Rome.

There were no pictures taken in Beirut. But there had

been so little time, of course, and David and Ellen had been honeymooning still, Bill had told Jan.

Beirut . . . Jan considered that thoughtfully.

Ellen and David in Beirut.

Jan decided that she must ask Ellen about her stay in the old Middle Eastern city.

Then her eyes went back to the picture of Ellen and Thalia together.

Looking at it, Jan gasped.

It was Thalia, yes, of course it was Thalia, whose hair was shorter than Ellen's, that was looking into the camera with love. Looking at David with love.

Ellen was partly turned aside.

Examining the picture carefully, Jan saw what Ellen must have been watching.

There was Ian, a tiny rim of reddish-gold head showing just within camera range, a sliver of big arm.

Ellen was looking at Ian.

Jan's hand shook as she gathered the pictures. She put them carefully into the file with the documents she kept there.

She had somehow, for a moment, mistaken Ellen and Thalia.

She had somehow switched them around in her mind.

Thalia's eyes, full of adoration . . .

And Ellen . . .

Jan shivered.

Could Ellen be dead?

Could Thalia, who wept for David, be alive?

Such a deception seemed improbably, hardly possible. The differences between the appearance of Ellen now, as opposed to when David had married her, could simply be a result of the stress of illness and grief.

Yet, the more Jan thought of it, the more her vague suspicion seemed not suspicion but fact.

The two girls had looked very much alike.

And golden hair could grow.

Ellen had come home, and died.

Thalia had taken her place as David's wife?

But why?

It could not have been for the inheritance.

No. Jan saw that quickly.

David had been young, healthy. No one could have foreseen his death.

If Ellen had come home and died, when David was living, nothing that he owned entered into it.

There would simply have been no sense to the deception.

She was, Jan told herself, allowing the whispering silence of the house to drive her into reckless speculations.

It was Ellen, it must be Ellen, who had wept for David in her arms. Ellen who wanted only to talk of him, think of him. Ellen who wore mourning black for him.

It must be Ellen.

Bill had seen her in Beirut. He would know if . . .

But Jan was not sure of Bill.

How did she know he had met Ellen in Beirut?

How did she know he had ever known David?

She squinted into the sunlight over the golden meadows, squeezing back quick hot tears, feeling as if she were entangled in an invisible web which was slowly tightening around her, tightening and drawing her into a final disaster.

It was only five days since the plump steward had hurried her off the train into the darkness before dawn, and Bill had come through slowly thinning shadows to meet her.

He had said then that Ellen was happy, excited, to know Jan was coming, and Jan, full of resentment, had wondered how Ellen could be happy after what had happened to David.

But Ellen had collapsed the moment she saw Jan, had collapsed into pitiful weeping, while Ian stood in the doorway, huge, golden, like a god out of an ancient myth.

Could Bill be concealing the fact that he knew the Ellen in Ballantine Lodge was not the Ellen that he had seen in Beirut?

Did he have some reason of his own for going along with a grotesque deception?

He had, at first, plainly tried to make her believe that

she was coming to a home like any other, though one touched by sorrow. He had become more candid later, said, "It's beginning now. First he wants to get rid of me."

Ian . . . the great golden god . . .

Jan shivered again. She wondered if David's feverish whispers, the five days in Ballantine Lodge, had simply addled her senses, driven her to search out hidden menace, some sick ugliness, where there was the tragedy of life unfolding itself as it always must to all men at some time or other.

Surely Ellen's grief was real. Her collapse real. Her love for David real.

And then, Jan thought that she had mistaken Thalia for Ellen only because of the adoration in Thalia's eyes. So Thalia had loved David, too.

Both sisters had loved him.

He had met Thalia first, hadn't he told Jan that? and then he'd met Ellen, and chosen her, but Thalia still loved him. Which explained her expression in the picture.

Jan told herself that it must have been Thalia who died. Yet a single stubborn thought remained in her mind. The girl who wore black, who mourned so honestly, actually could be Thalia.

Jan turned away from the blue-draped window, turned away from her confused thoughts. She went into the hallway.

The door to Mrs. Ballantine's room was closed now.

Jan went to it, tapped lightly.

Vera opened it, grinned, "You don't mind taking punishment, do you? But she's sleeping again. And I'm not kidding." Vera stepped back. "Take a look."

Mrs. Ballantine, propped on her pillows, looked like a tiny mummy left in an airless tomb.

"See what I mean? He was here. It's always like that, you know?" Vera sighed. "I sure wish I had somebody to talk to. What a job."

"Does Ellen ever come up?"

"Her? Hah!"

"Never?"

"Not since I've been here. Some daughter is all I can

say." Vera glanced at Mrs. Ballantine's still form. "Though it sure doesn't matter, does it?"

Jan agreed that it didn't matter. She supposed that Ellen, distraught over her loss, found it too much of a strain to see her mother.

"I'll come and talk to you later," Jan told Vera, and went down the hallway, past the stairs to the wing beyond, to the wing where the others had their rooms.

She had never gone that way before. She saw that it was a duplicate of the wing in which she stayed.

A long carpeted corridor, dim and shadowy with blue reflected from floor and walls, and darker blue doors.

Jan didn't know which room was Ellen's, but she hoped to be able to find it.

She hoped that she could steal a moment with Ellen, a moment alone with her, without the overwhelming presence of Ian and his watchful blue flame eyes.

But, though the long carpeted hallway muffled her own quick light footsteps, it seemed to act as a funnel for sudden voices.

Jan heard the words clearly.

Ian said, his words low, hard, menacing, "But where did you get the key, Ellen?"

"I found it," Ellen cried. "I just found it, I tell you."

And even Jan, freezing against the wall, sensed that was not the truth.

"Who gave it to you, Ellen? I want to know. I mean to know. Who gave you that key?"

"Nobody, Ian. Nobody, I swear."

"Do you know what you did? Do you understand? Jan saw you there that night. She was wandering around, I don't know why, and she saw you. I found her there, looking at you while you slept. While you slept in that room, Ellen."

"I couldn't help it, Ian. I have to sleep. I have to."

"You won't go in there any more. You've seen the new lock. And I have the only key. That's the end of that. Don't even try, Ellen. Do you hear me. You're to forget it. So don't even try."

"But it's Thalia's room. I need to . . . I have to . . . sometimes I think I'm . . ."

"Forget it, Ellen."

Hard emphasis. *Ellen.*

Jan heard it, shivered against the wall, but couldn't move.

"I'm trying to, Ian, but . . ."

"You're not trying hard enough. Forget it, Ellen, Ellen . . . Ellen . . ."

The voices died away.

A door opened.

Jan forced herself away from the wall. She turned, raced back the way she had come. At the steps, she stopped, kneeled down, pretended to be adjusting her shoe.

Ian was coming, coming.

She heard the thud of his footsteps on the thick blue carpet. She kept her head down, fingers busy at her shoe.

He mustn't know that she had overheard him talking to Ellen. He mustn't even suspect it.

He said, "Is something wrong, Jan?"

She glanced up then, gave her shoe a final touch, smiled at him, and rose. "Oh, no. I just caught my heel. But I think it's all right. Not broken or anything."

"You want to be careful. You don't want to fall down the steps and hurt yourself."

"Oh, I won't," she assured him, and wondered if she were imagining what she sensed to be a threat in his words.

The overheard conversation between him and Ellen echoed in her mind. The fear in Ellen, the menace in Ian.

Why didn't he want her to go to Thalia's room?

Why had someone told her, was it Vera or Mrs. Mayor, that room had been Ellen's?

Aloud Jan asked, "How's Ellen now, Ian?"

"She'll be down for dinner." He took Jan's arm. "Come on, let's have a drink together. I seem to be always too occupied with my responsibilities to spend any time with you. And I'm sorry for that."

They sat on the terrace. He on the wall, looking down at her. She on one of the white leatherette chairs.

For a little while, they were simply relatives, in-laws, sharing casual talk over gin and tonic.

He seemed a big, somewhat tired man, over-burdened at thirty-five, with family problems, rather than any of the things she had imagined about him.

But then, thinking of the pictures she had been looking at earlier, she said, "You must miss Carl very much, Ian."

"Of course I do."

"Doesn't he ever come home?"

"He hasn't for some time." Ian paused. Then, "I've been to see him, but since . . ."

"Yes," she said quickly. "I understand. I would so like to know him, too. He must be very sweet."

"He's only seventeen. I would like him to remain untouched, unscarred by all this . . ."

"And by the Ballantine curse?"

Ian nodded. "Something like that is what I was thinking."

"When I go East, Ian, I could visit him. You did say Carl's at school in the East, didn't you?"

Ian nodded. "Yes. But . . ."

"And where?"

Ian's blue flame eyes looked at her, then away. "You wouldn't know the place. It's very small. Not advertised. I want him to have simple surroundings, you see. I don't believe in the trappings." Ian went on, describing the school, the theory behind it, the kind of boys there.

But he didn't, Jan noticed, mention the name of the school, or where it was.

It seemed a curious omission, a deliberate evasion. She asked herself why Ian so definitely did not want her to go to visit Carl.

The brief silence that had fallen when Ian stopped talking prolonged itself for too long.

She could feel him watching her. She couldn't think of anything to say.

Finally, trying to maintain the sense of family talking together, trying to get back to it and out of the muted threat in the too-long silence, Jan said, "I was glad I had the chance to visit your mother today, Ian. I wondered, when I saw her, if you'd ever thought of therapy for her. There is such a lot that can be done for people who have had strokes. And somehow . . ."

"Yes," he asked softly. "And somehow . . ."

But Jan hesitated. She realized suddenly that she had made a mistake. She didn't want to tell Ian that she suspected Mrs. Ballantine could hear, understand, could possibly be gotten to communicate.

She didn't, in that moment, dare to stop and examine her reason for feeling that way. She was too afraid that anything she thought might show on her face, that Ian might be able to read it in her mind.

It was Bill who came to her rescue.

He walked onto the terrace, grinning. "You two certainly make a pretty pair in the sunset."

"Do we?" Ian eyed Bill without amusement. Then turned to Jan. "I hope you think so, too, Jan."

She didn't answer him.

She couldn't. Whenever he turned on that too-obvious charm, whenever he smiled at her in that particular way, she froze.

Bill said, "I have struck her, or is it I had stricken her? speechless."

She gave him an exasperated look.

In the brief silence, a blue and white bird settled on the terrace wall, and tipped back its head, and trilled a great long symphony of sweet notes into the still air.

It seemed to spill a mist of magic over Jan.

She raised her face, smiling.

And then Ian clapped his hands.

Chapter 11

THE SOUND he made was like an explosive gun shot. The quick sharp report abruptly snapped off the sweet trilling song, and tore to shreds the mist of magic.

The blue and white bird wings spread and the bird soared away, disappearing into the red rocks below.

And Jan, wishing that she, too, could fly away from Ballantine Lodge, found herself shrinking on the white leatherette chair.

There was another brief silence.

It ended on a distant, muted cry. A wail that rose and faded so quickly that it might never have rippled through the air.

But it had been real.

For Ian was on his feet, shrugging tiredly, "That's Ellen again." He shot a blue flame look at Jan, and hurried indoors.

Jan said dryly, "I guess I don't get a chance to talk to Ellen tonight."

"Did you expect to?"

She stared at Bill. "Why not? Sooner or later I will."

"Maybe."

"I will," she repeated.

He turned to look at her, his big, almost hooked nose, his deep-set eyes, expressing masculine disapproval. "You can be very self-assertive, can't you, Jan?"

"I have to be. Some time it's completely necessary."

"It can also be . . . well, look, it can be dangerous, too, Jan."

She instantly leaned forward, "Tell me in what way."

He shrugged.

"But I'll have to see Ellen before I leave here. No matter how long it takes."

"You've already seen her. You could have been gone by now. You're stalling, Jan. You're stalling, and you're not fooling me any more than you're fooling Ian."

But she was thinking of that muted cry, the long sad wail, abruptly broken off, that had drawn Ian indoors.

"Could that have been Ellen crying out?" she asked Bill.

"It must have been."

She watched his dark eyes. " 'Must have been.' But could it have been anyone else?"

"Mrs. Ballantine, for instance? Is that what you're driving at?"

Jan thought of what Vera had told her. Vera had thought that she heard a cry while Mrs. Ballantine was alone. Ian had come in, sent Vera out of the room, and after that, Mrs. Ballantine had slept for days.

Mrs. Ballantine had slept for days after Ian had gone to her room.

Jan said slowly, "You don't know what I'm driving at, Bill?"

"I heard you suggesting the therapy bit to Ian. You must have had a reason for bringing that up to him. You did, didn't you?"

Jan shook her head.

"Sure you did. And you didn't fool him any more than you can fool me. You had a feeling that she wasn't actually as paralyzed as Ian had led you to believe, didn't you?"

"Have you ever seen Mrs. Ballantine, Bill?"

"No. I haven't."

"Could I be imagining it?"

He sighed. "Listen, Jan, please don't play busy-body. Don't take any more chances than you already have. Just get yourself out of here."

"To leave you a clear field?" she demanded.

His face hardened. "All right. If you want to put it that way. Yes. To leave me a clear field."

She shook her head. "I refuse to make it that easy for you."

"You certainly do."

"Then tell me what it's all about, Bill."

"Why? Why should I? And why do you insist on involving yourself in what is obviously not your concern?"

"Not my concern!" she flared. "You have a strange sense of values, don't you? Ellen *is* my concern. Yes. Mine. I can't see any way in which she is yours."

"You can't?"

Jan said unwillingly, "Well, perhaps I can . . . "

"At least it isn't money," he said softly. "You know that. I'm not after her money. But you . . . ? What about you, Jan? Isn't that why you came here? Aren't you just trying to keep Ellen from . . ."

The suggestion seemed to strike through Jan, a swift painful blow under which she winced and gasped. She jumped to her feet. She knew that she ought to tell him about Ellen's letters to David. She knew that it was the right moment to explain about her suspicions, mad as they seemed, even to her. Yet she cried, "Just call me the Mercer Monster, Bill," and fled indoors.

She wore white that evening. A slim-waisted dress that flared around her knees, narrow pumps that showed off her slender ankles.

Vera, peeping at her from the room at the end of the hall, had grinned approval.

Mrs. Mayor bounced into the foyer to cry, "Why, Jan, dear, how lovely," blue eyes beaming from her plump face. "Why, dear, yes, you do look lovely."

So far, Jan told herself, so good.

It had been a ploy, which seemed to her, in the privacy of her room, a definite step forward. Vera, and then Mrs. Mayor, seemed to confirm the judgment.

But when Jan reached the living room, when Ian came to meet her, his blue flame eyes aglow, and his craggy face broken in a wide smile, she decided that she had made a mistake.

She knew that she could not learn the truth about Ballantine Lodge by charming Ian into a susceptible, or unwary, state. He was one step ahead of her always, she saw helplessly, in a game for which he himself had set the rules.

The answer, for her, was to refuse to play.

But, dressed as she was, dimpled, smiling in her entrance, she had committed herself.

Ian came to meet her. "You are lovely, Jan."

And as she thanked him, she saw Bill's disapproving dark eyes narrow, and saw his face tighten.

She thanked Ian, accepted the drink he brought to her.

The table was set for three again.

She decided that she wouldn't mention Ellen.

But Ian said, "I'm afraid my poor sister can't join us tonight, Jan. It's a shame, really. I had hoped that she would begin to improve by now."

"I hoped so, too." Jan smiled into Ian's eyes. "You don't really think, do you, Ian, that *I* upset Ellen?"

He seemed to hesitate before the appealing gray gaze. Then, "It's the situation, of course, Jan . . . but as I did tell you . . ."

"If you want me to go . . ." She let the words trail away in wistfulness. "But I did so hope . . . Still, the lawyers could easily take over."

Past Ian's massive shoulder, she saw the sudden grin soften Bill's face.

Ian said, "I only want what's best for Ellen, for all of us, Jan. I'm sure you know that."

She thought again that there were two conversations going at the same time. One spoken, one unspoken, yet understood.

She said deliberately, "Of course you do, Ian. So do I." She waited for a moment. Then, "And very soon, unless Ellen shows some improvement, you must let me call a doctor in. We can't let this go on and on, you know."

His face hardened, but he said, "She just needs more time, Jan. I won't let anyone say . . . "

". . . That Ellen is mentally ill?" Jan looked, with what she hoped was innocence into Ian's eyes. "But illness is illness. What difference does it make how you name it?"

Bill got to his feet, his lean body relaxed, yet moving

with quick grace. "You seem to need a refill, Jan." Then, "And you, Ian?"

Ian nodded.

Bill brought the Martini pitcher, and Jan held her glass out to him.

As he poured the clear liquid into it, he said, "There. I think that's quite enough, don't you?"

The house had settled into midnight silence.

Jan had gone to bed early, hoping to fall quickly into the escape of sleep.

But sleep would not come. She finally gave up wooing it, and abandoned herself to uneasy wakefulness.

She prowled the darkness of her room, until, drawn by pale moonlight to the window, she stared out on the great sea of silver pampas grass, looked eastward to friends, and home, and safety, and wondered if she would ever know them again.

But she had promised David . . .

It was a promise that must be kept.

And beyond the promise to David, there were the almost-understood words that she heard in the whispering silence.

She couldn't turn her back and flee, even though her every instinct told her she must. She was beginning, she knew, to believe in the Ballantine curse. In Ian's curse.

And Ellen?

Mrs. Ballantine?

Jan went to the closet. She took down the file, slipped the pictures from it, and examined them again under the pale light of the bed lamp.

Ian and Carl . . .

Why had Ian been so vague about the school to which he had sent Carl?

Why didn't Ian want her to visit Carl?

She decided that it must be because he was one of the group that had been in Rome when Ellen met David.

Thalia had been one, and she was dead.

Carl had been one, and he was away somewhere.

Sarah Jarvis had been one, and she, too, was away somewhere.

David . . .

Only Ian and Ellen were left.

And Ellen. . . .

Jan sighed and put the pictures away, suddenly overwhelmed by a sense of aloneness. She had been raised to be self-sufficient, she reminded herself. She had always been able to take care of herself. She always would be. And yet . . . now she wished she had a strong arm to lean on. She wished she had someone to talk to.

She thought of Bill, and rejected the thought.

She turned away from the closet, meaning to go back to bed.

But she heard something outside.

Instantly, she went to the window, pressed against the screen to look down.

She saw empty moonlight shining on the empty terrace. Below the stone wall, she saw sharp-edged shadows, the rocks on which Thalia had flung herself and died.

And then there was a sudden movement in the moonlight. A tall lean shadow moved slowly across the terrace, and turned and came back again. A tall lean shadow . . . silver moonlight on dark hair, on an uptilted face.

Bill.

Bill, prowling through the shadows of the terrace.

Jan watched him for a moment.

Then she snatched her robe, stepped into slippers.

She didn't stop to think because she didn't want to think.

She needed someone to talk to, to lean on.

Bill had known David.

Bill was a link to that reality which seemed then to be fast slipping away from Jan forever.

She scurried down the hall, tripped, stumbled, and skipped her way on the steps.

The silent house whispered around her.

It was as if it had been emptied forever of life.

There was nothing left but the darkness within, the silver sky without.

She pulled the door open, hurtled onto the terrace, hands out, beseeching, the words ready on her lips.

But the terrace was empty.

Bill was gone.

A breeze moved in the cedars, and sent a furry shadow drifting on the red stone wall.

Jan whispered, "Bill? Where are you, Bill?"

Nothing.

No one.

She turned slowly. She studied the shadowy corners of the terrace. She took a few steps one way, then another, hesitating in bewilderment.

She had seen Bill. She had seen his lean shadow, seen his face tilted up, touched by silver moonlight.

"Bill?" she whispered again.

There was no answer.

At last, she turned to go indoors.

She brushed a wrought-iron chair, and stumbled and caught herself.

And at the same time, she saw rising from the white leatherette cushion a strange wavering dark coil.

She saw the dark coil rising, rippling. She heard an odd sound, the scattering of pebbles on stone.

She flung herself back and away until she hit the terrace wall, and the black coil seemed to move with her. It came lancing upward off the white cushion, and struck and fell away.

She felt the swift sting burn into her shoulder.

The black coil at her feet became an odd humping ribbon that streaked into the darkness.

She clung to the terrace wall and screamed.

Chapter 12

THE SCREAM rose, spread, shrill with mindless terror. It went on and on and on in great building echoes.

She was frozen against the terrace wall, trapped in spinning darkness, with her throat straining to make the terrible sound that she heard as if it were no part of her at all, and her hand pressed to her shoulder where the black coil struck and left a swift stinging that burned through her flesh.

The wings of the house suddenly bloomed with light that streamed onto the terrace.

The door crashed open.

Bill came. He seemed to dive across the distance between them.

He was in the doorway, in movement, and then Jan was in his arms.

He was saying words she couldn't understand.

He was holding her and whispering.

Then he shook her. He shook her so hard that her head snapped back and forth on her shoulders, and the dark spun around her, and at last, the terrible echoing screams stopped, and she realized that she, her straining throat, had been making that awful sound.

Still in his arms, aware of the sudden silence, she was aware, too, of his heart beating against her, aware of his touch.

"Tell me what happened," he demanded, his voice harsh, angry.

She gasped, fought for control. She shivered, and sobbed, and finally, she managed to whisper, "It was there. I saw it, Bill. It was on the chair. And it came up . . ."

"What, Jan?"

"A snake. It looked black. It was coiled, waiting. It rose up. It . . ."

He seemed to understand then. He jerked her hand from her shoulder. He pulled at her robe, and it tore under his impatient fingers. At the same time, he was moving her, thrusting her towards the door, closer to the light.

She could hear him murmuring, and realized that what she heard was the slow unreeling of emphatic curses that dropped unceasingly from his almost-bloodless lips.

He bent his dark head. He stared at the two tiny marks on her shoulder. Two pin pricks, and two dots of blood. He stroked them away with a careful finger, and poked and probed, searching for something around the small wounds.

At last he raised his head. "There's no swelling. No venom." He grinned at her, relief flowering in his eyes.

But she couldn't stop shaking. She leaned against him, her knees weak, hardly holding her up. "It made a noise. I heard it, Bill. As it came up from the chair, it . . . it rattled."

He turned then, and she realized for the first time that Ian and Mrs. Mayor were crowded in the doorway with them.

Crowded there, and talking, and reaching for her, as if they had been there ever since her screams began but she hadn't known it, hadn't heard their frantic questions, nor even seen them.

Bill moved her, turned her and settled her in Mrs. Mayor's plump receiving arms, ignoring Jan's small sound of protest.

He jerked his head, and Mrs. Mayor said, "Yes, yes, oh, yes," in a high thin voice, and then, leading Jan indoors. "Snakes! My dear, whatever next. Imagine to find a snake on the terrace." She pressed Jan into a corner of the sofa, and stood back. "Brandy. Yes, indeed. Brandy, I think. And for me, too!"

"By all means," Ian agreed. "Brandy all around." He turned blue flame eyes on Jan, eyes that regarded her with mixed annoyance and amusement. "What were you doing on the terrace in the middle of the night, Jan?"

But she didn't answer him. She fixed her eyes on the door. Bill hadn't come in. She was waiting for him. She could hear movements, his footsteps, the grate of wrought-iron furniture. She wondered what he was doing.

"We've never had snakes here before," Ian told her. "Not on the terrace. They'd hardly venture so near the house."

Jan pressed her hand to her shoulder, a mute reminder that what had never happened before had nevertheless happened that night.

"I'm sorry," he went on. "I wouldn't have wanted to see you so frightened." His voice dropped. "Not for anything, Jan."

From outside, she heard a crash, the sound of blows. She was on her feet without knowing that she had moved.

Mrs. Mayor, pouring brandy, cried, "What now?" and almost dropped the bottle.

Ian smiled. "I believe the hunter must have found his prey." And then, coolly to Mrs. Mayor, "Will you do that? Or shall I?"

Unaccustomly silent, she brought a glass to Jan, one to Ian. When Bill came in moments later, she handed him a glass, too. Then she stood watching, her blue eyes faintly worried as they shifted back and forth between Ian and Bill.

"All right?" Bill asked Jan, and when she nodded, "I got it."

"An unnecessary kill," Ian said smoothly. "It would surely have been frightened away by the noise and light."

"Well, I'm delighted," Mrs. Mayor cried, clutching her blue cotton robe around her plump waist. "I wouldn't have slept a wink. Not ever. Not in this house. But now . . ." She raised her blue eyes to the ceiling, as if in sudden recollection, "And can you imagine? They never heard a thing . . . why, Ellen, and Vera . . ."

Jan stopped listening. She had just noticed that Mrs. Mayor was wearing a robe, that both Bill and Ian were in shirt sleeves and trousers, as if neither of them had been to bed yet.

It was as if lost memory had suddenly come back.

Her heart began to thud against her ribs. Small shivers shook her. She wondered if her legs would hold her. She wondered if she would even be able to get upstairs, to the seclusion, the safety, of her room, before the last remnants of her strength deserted her.

Bill came over to her, put out his hand. "I think we should disinfect your shoulder, Jan. And then you ought to get some rest."

Because lost memory had come back, she cringed, and shook her head.

He had been on the terrace. She saw him, his face lifted in the pale moonlight. She had wanted to talk to him, to tell him everything she knew, to ask his help. She had hurried down, through the silent house, only to find him gone.

But the snake had been there, a black coil on the white cushion.

It had been there, awaiting her unwary approach.

Bill . . .

What did she know of him?

Why had she thought, for those few moments earlier, that she dare trust him?

He seemed to know what she was thinking. He stared at her for a long silent moment, then shrugged and turned away.

"Come along," Mrs. Mayor said. "Come along, dear, do. We'll see to your shoulder, and tuck you away into bed."

Mrs. Mayor, yawning, had finally left her.

The pin pricks, washed with alcohol, were covered with tape.

The room was dark and still.

Jan was in bed, adrift somewhere between wakefulness and sleep. There was a faint tap at the door. She came up with a convulsive start, smothering a cry in her raw throat.

The door opened, framing a tall, lean shadow.

She recognized Bill instantly, and demanded, "What do you want?"

He came in, closed the door behind him. He stopped well away from her, said, "Jan, lest you're still worried, I examined the snake after I killed it. It had no venom at all. It had been milked dry."

"Milked dry?" she whispered. "But what does that mean?"

"It wasn't intended to kill you. Only to frighten you."

"Only to frighten me," she echoed.

"Why did you come down to the terrace?"

She didn't answer him.

He waited. Then, "Did you see me there?"

"I did, yes," she said finally.

"You think that I left the snake, waited for you to see me, then slipped indoors?"

"You could have, Bill."

"Yes. But I didn't. I heard something outside, went down to have a look. I didn't see anything wrong, so I went into the house, prowled around."

"Then Ian . . . ?"

"Pack up and get out," Bill told her. "Do it tomorrow, Jan."

She tasted the cold bitter flavor of fear.

Bill wanted her to go away.

The black coil, with no venom, rising . . .

She said finally, swallowing against the soreness in her throat, "Maybe it was an accident, one of those rare things that happen some times."

"Maybe it was," he agreed.

But he didn't sound convinced.

And she, watching him turn and leave the room, didn't feel convinced.

The next morning, even though her shoulder was still taped, her throat still raw, it was as if those screaming moments in the moonlight had been no more than an extended nightmare.

Ian was waiting for her, black coffee poured and ready, when she came down.

He looked admiringly at her short-sleeved dress of cedar green, asked, "And how are you today, Jan?"

But she knew that he was not referring to her terror of the night before. It was, simply, his usual morning greeting.

She said, "I'm sorry I disturbed your rest last night, Ian."

His blue flame eyes flicked at her, a quick searing glance. "It was an odd thing to happen. But such things do." Then, "Perhaps you'd like to go into Mercer with me for a little while." He bent over to refill her coffee cup. "It might be a bit of a diversion for you. Not . . ." he added in his most smooth voice, ". . . that it can compare to the world you know, the world you must miss so much while you are here, Jan. But still . . . to escape this house for a short time . . ."

She thanked him but refused.

To escape the house, yes, that was what she most wanted. To escape the whispering silence.

But with him gone, there might be the opportunity to talk to Ellen alone, an opportunity to visit with Mrs. Ballantine.

He smiled at Jan as if he knew what she had been thinking. "There'll be practically nothing for you to do."

She didn't have to answer.

Mrs. Mayor came bouncing in, dark blue dotted swiss swirling around her. "Oh, there you are," she cried, her blue eyes worried. "You must do something about Vera, Ian. Since last night . . . oh, I suppose I oughtn't to have told her, but it just slipped out, and since then . . . snakes, oh, dear. The very thought . . . but Vera, she's using it as an excuse, of course. She is so lonely, Ian. Don't you think? Someone from the village perhaps? A few hours break? It is hard, do think of it, the poor child . . ."

Ian frowned. "She's paid well enough."

"But she's young, Ian." Mrs. Mayor appealed to Jan. "You do understand, don't you? Vera . . . really, she is so young."

"I'll see about it when I'm in Mercer. Yes, perhaps I can find someone to come in for a few hours a week at least." His voice went harsh. "But to have strangers around . . . to have our problems aired over half the state . . ." He smiled at Jan. "You see? There's always something. What about it then? Will you come along?"

Once again, she refused.

In a little while, Bill came down.

The three of them had breakfast together, and it was still as if those screaming moments in the moonlight had been no more than a nightmare.

He gave her a quick look, greeted her, then retreated into silence.

The meal done, they separated.

Jan was in her room, watching from the blue-draped window, when she saw the big black limousine back slowly from its parking place below the terrace.

It was, she realized, the first time since her arrival, the first time in six days, that Ian had left the house.

Soon after, Bill's smaller car drove away.

She wondered briefly if he were following Ian, and if so, why. Then she thought that Bill could easily be off on errands of his own.

But she decided not to waste precious time in speculation. Now was her opportunity to be with Ellen, to speak to her without the witnessing presence of Ian.

Jan slipped down the hall, turned into the far wing. It was very quiet. She paused, listening before Ellen's door. There wasn't a sound. Nothing, nothing but the whispering silence in which Jan heard words she could almost understand.

She tapped lightly. There was no answer.

She called Ellen's name. Nothing happened.

She tried the door, and found it locked.

Again she tapped, and waited for an answer.

She waited, knowing that she would hear nothing. But at last, she turned away. She hurried downstairs.

She found Mrs. Mayor in the kitchen, asked breathlessly, "Do you have a key to Ellen's room?"

"A key?" Blue eyes stared at her from a plump face. "A key to Ellen's room, dear. What do you mean?"

Jan said, fighting for patience, "Ellen's locked into her room. I want to talk to her. I have to talk to her, Mrs. Mayor."

Mrs. Mayor nodded, plainly unsurprised. "Yes, he will do that sometimes. When Ellen . . ." She paused. "You want to talk to her, dear? Oh, yes, of course you do. And you do mean *her* room, don't you? You see, I was confused. There's Ellen's room in Ian's wing, and then there's the one across the hall from you. That's what Ian called it anyway. But the room in your wing was really Thalia's room. And what a to do there was over that! I had the key, and poor Ellen wanted it, so I gave it to her. What harm is there in that? And then . . . well, Ian . . ." Mrs. Mayor's plump shoulders heaved, "Forgive me dear, but he can be unreasonable. So I just never mentioned it to him . . . Not that it mattered . . . He changed the lock anyway, didn't he?"

"But the key to the room where Ellen is now," Jan asked.

"Let me think. Yes. It will be here some place."

No amount of urging could make the housekeeper hurry, but at last, she found what she was looking for in a silver drawer, and put it into Jan's hand. "Mind now. He doesn't know about this one. I expect it's from Sarah Jarvis' old set. I don't care to remind him either."

Jan nodded, hurried upstairs. There was still no sound from behind the locked door.

Jan turned the key, went in.

Ellen was lying on the bed, her slender body limp under a sheet, her pale face turned into the pillow.

She was asleep, sunk in the slow, still sleep of the drugged.

Jan watched her hopelessly, then backed out, re-locked the door.

She couldn't talk to Ellen.

Ian had known that she wouldn't be able to. He had gone into Mercer only after having ordered his house behind him.

The faint pattern that drifted beneath the shadow of Mercer Mountain seemed to sharpen.

Ian was determined to keep Jan from spending more than a few moments with Ellen. He wanted the papers signed, but he did not want to urge Jan too directly to finish her business with Ellen.

He pretended to want Jan to stay, and yet ... ?

The black coil on the white chair ...

Bill had told her that the snake's venom had been drawn. It had been meant to frighten, not to injure her.

But she had seen Bill, Bill, not Ian, on the terrace the night before.

Did each of them have separate reasons for wanting her gone from Ballantine Lodge?

Jan returned the key to Mrs. Mayor.

"Did you speak to her, dear? Is she all right?"

Jan shook her head.

"Sleeping, was she? Poor child, she does need her rest, doesn't she? She does sleep too much in my opinion though."

Jan didn't answer.

She went upstairs.

Vera, standing in the half-opened doorway at the end of the hall, cried, "I saw him go away. What are you doing? Come keep me company."

Jan smiled. "Now that's a good idea."

"Mrs. Ballantine is out cold. You don't even have to whisper." Vera shook her sandy head. "I mean it. Really out cold."

Ellen, Jan thought. Ellen was gone into a drugged sleep and unreachable.

And Mrs. Ballantine ... ?

Jan followed Vera into the shadowy room.

Vera asked, "Okay if I have a cigarette first, while I have the chance?"

Jan nodded, and walked around the bed.

Mrs. Ballantine lay set among the pillows, her tiny old face as loose as melted wax, her brace-locked hands tucked against her sides.

Jan pulled a chair close, sat down. Instinctively, she put her hand on the old woman's withered arm. It was a gesture of compassion, unconsciously offered, and with no expectation of recognition.

But very slowly, Mrs. Ballantine's melted wax face

seemed to tighten. Her thin lashes stirred, and fluttered. Her wrinkled, blue-veined lids rose, revealing drug-clouded hazel eyes.

Jan whispered, "Don't be afraid of me. Trust me. I know something's wrong. I want to help you, to help Ellen."

Mrs. Ballantine's drug-clouded eyes seemed to clear. They showed awakening consciousness, and with it, the sharp edge of terror. They shifted from Jan's face to the door, then back again.

"Yes?" Jan whispered.

Mrs. Ballantine's wrinkled lips writhed. Her wrinkled throat worked. Then she brought out a single, hoarse word. "David."

"David?" Jan repeated, bewildered.

"Beautiful. Both beautiful. One love. One stone . . ."

Jan breathed, "Mrs. Ballantine . . ."

But cloudiness had settled again in the old lady's hazel eyes focused so sharply on Jan's face. The cloudiness was there as her wrinkled lips strained again, saying, "No. No. Thalia."

Jan, not understanding, leaned closer. She pressed her lips to Mrs. Ballantine's cheek in a gentle kiss. "Tell me."

"David," Mrs. Ballantine whispered.

And a bar of light fell across the bed.

Vera cried, "Is *she* talking, Jan?"

Jan rose quickly, went to Vera. "Of course not."

Vera stared at the old lady, "I could of sworn . . . just like that time . . ."

Jan forced herself to grin. "I was probably talking to myself."

"This place can lead you to it. What I wouldn't give for some fun. I mean, nothing spectacular. Just a movie, a beer in town, you know?"

"If you hate it so much, why do you stay, Vera?"

Vera shrugged, tossed her sandy head. "Well, it's my first job. He got me through school, wrote to them, you know? You can imagine the reference he'd give me if I walked off. And anyhow, let's face it, I don't have fare back to Minnesota, which is where I come from. The way he worked it, and that was smart of him believe me, he banks my pay for me. I'm building up a pretty penny for when the job is over. But right now . . ."

"He said he'd see if he could find someone to hire in Mercer to come out and spell you."

Vera grinned. "Fat chance. That was just to shut Mrs. Mayor up, I'll bet you. He doesn't want anybody else around. Crazy guy, Ian Ballantine. Crazy, you know?"

Chapter 13

JAN SAT at the window, her eyes fixed in an unseeing gaze on the eastern horizon.

She thought that it was impossible to make sense out of Mrs. Ballantine's incoherent words, yet they kept echoing through Jan's mind.

David . . .

Beautiful, both beautiful . . . one love, one stone.

No. Thalia.

But Mrs. Ballantine had been left at home, an invalid who couldn't travel, Ian had said, while he took his sisters and Carl, with Sarah Jarvis as chaperone, on the trip which had finally led them to David.

Mrs. Ballantine had never met David. Then why had she mentioned his name?

David . . .

Beautiful, both beautiful . . . One love, one stone.

No. Thalia.

David.

A swift cold shiver rippled through Jan.

Mrs. Ballantine could speak. She had said those words. Her hazel eyes had looked into Jan's pleadingly, and full of horror.

But Ian had said from the very beginning that the old lady was mute, paralyzed, beyond response or understanding, that she had been that way for many years.

Yet she did speak, she understood. She had known who Jan was, and shown it by saying David's name.

David . . .

Beautiful, both beautiful . . . one love, one stone.

No. Thalia.

Ellen and Thalia . . . both beautiful.

One with a heart of love. One with a heart of stone. Another swift cold shiver rippled through Jan.

Ian had taken Sarah Jarvis, not Mrs. Ballantine, on the trip with his family.

Sarah . . .

Sarah, who had been sent away from the Lodge just about a month before. Sarah, Mrs. Mayor said, was too old, too tired to cope with an invalid, a sick-hearted girl, a big house. But Mrs. Mayor had never known Sarah Jarvis. Her words were simply repetitions of what Ian told her.

When Mrs. Mayor was hired, she found a drugged, dazed, speechless old woman, immobilized by braces, by fear, in a room soon guarded by a young, inexperienced practical nurse chosen by mail from far away.

Jan saw the truth with sudden intuitive sharpness.

There was no Mrs. Ballantine.

It was Sarah Jarvis who had spoken to her, looked at her pleadingly from dazed, horror-filled hazel eyes.

Sarah Jarvis, who twice crying out, perhaps in a drug-induced nightmare, had brought Ian to his feet and hurrying into the house.

He, with his frequent solitary visits to the old woman's bedside, must somehow ensure her silence. Her silence.

Jan asked herself what the old woman knew that she must not say, but couldn't find the answer.

And below her, the black limousine crept along the curves of the dusty pink road, disappeared momentarily into the green shadows of the cedars, and then pulled, like a ship into port, into the parking area below the terrace.

Ian got out. He paused there for a moment, looking up at the house.

She shrank back, feeling as if his blue flame eyes could sear her.

The sun glowed in his red-gold hair, touched the smoothly brushed waves with fire. His big hands were behind him. His wide shoulders, great barrel chest, were rigid, as hard as the red rock of Mercer Mountain. The red shadow of Mercer Mountain.

He was like a great golden god out of an ancient myth, she thought, as she had thought before. A god out of an ancient myth of evil, moving arrogantly among men, and plotting to destroy them.

Now he came up the stone steps slowly, and below, beyond him, a pink cloud moved on the road.

Jan watched it draw near, then nearer. Soon she recognized Bill's car.

She wondered if he had been following Ian. Then thought that they might have gone separately into town so that they could talk together, unheard, unobserved.

Bill and Ian could easily be partners in . . . in what? Why keep an old woman helpless? And Ellen . . .

But Bill had looked at Ellen with pity . . . with . . . yes, Jan told herself, with what could have been love.

Jan watched him get out of the car. Tall, lithe. He, too, paused at the foot of the stone steps. He, too, looked up, his face shadowed.

Once again she moved back from the window. She remembered his arms around her, his deep voice unreeling harsh curses as he looked at the blood-dotted pin pricks on her shoulder.

There had been tenderness in him then. She had felt it even through her terror. His tenderness had been a caress, his arms holding her an embrace.

She yearned to feel it again, and was disgusted at her heart's treachery.

Bill had been on the terrace. He said he went out to investigate some sound, and found nothing, and returned to the house. And a few moments later, she had seen the black coil rising from the white cushion.

She was surrounded by enemies, with no one to trust, no one to turn to.

Ellen . . .

Ian . . .

And what about Mrs. Mayor?

What about Vera?

Jan didn't even know for certain that she could trust

the small, defenceless woman who lay in the room down
the hall. Perhaps her whispered words had been the
product of derangement. Perhaps she *was* Mrs. Ballantine.

Jan sighed. The still room was a prison, a draped,
waxed, sun-filled prison. Yet she did not want to leave it.

Bill said that the snake, its venom drawn, had been
meant to send her in headlong flight from Ballantine
Lodge.

It was what he wanted. What Ian wanted.

She did not want to look into Bill's face.

She did not want to look into Ian's smiling blue flame
eyes.

But in a little while, Mrs. Mayor came tapping at the
door, carrying Ian's summons. "He's asking for you, Jan.
You must come down, do. He's back from Mercer and
and wanting to know how you are." Mrs. Mayor's blue
eyes anxiously searched Jan's face. "You are all right,
dear? No bad effects from last night after all? We were
so worried. Snakes! What next? And on the terrace, too!"

"I'm fine." Jan managed a smile. "There's just two
tiny pin pricks to show for all the noise I made."

Mrs. Mayor chuckled. "Noise? Why, my dear, I thought
the house would go tumbling down the mountain. But if
it had been me . . ." her plump shoulders quivered. "I
do believe I would have thrown myself off the terrace."

Jan thought that Bill might have been quite wrong.
Perhaps she, as Mrs. Mayor suggested now, was supposed to have thrown herself from the terrace to escape
the black coil rising with the sound of scattering pebbles.

Perhaps she was to have died as Thalia died.

Mrs. Mayor cried, "But you are really quite pale, dear."

"Is Ellen downstairs?"

"Ellen? Why, no, poor child. She's in her room.
Though I tell you, I think he does worry about her too
much. Really, a most peculiar man in some ways. How
he went on about the key to the room. Why, dear, ri-
diculous. It wouldn't hurt Ellen to visit her old room. But
no, no. I'll tell you, dear, because I do trust your discretion. Why, I gave Ellen the key myself. I suppose it was

another one of those that Sarah Jarvis left behind. I did give it to Ellen. But I thought it best not to say that. And Ellen, sweet love, she didn't give me away. But then, the very next morning, a new brass lock on the door. That man is odd, Jan. And I do think, if he would just leave her alone a bit instead of talking at her all the time she would do much better." Mrs. Mayor paused briefly, breathing hard.

"Yes . . ." Jan murmured.

"She's had a terrible loss. I know. I know. Dear Jan, I've had the same loss myself. One does not forget a husband in three weeks or four, or three years or four. But still . . . still . . . if he would just leave her alone."

"I've thought much the same thing myself," Jan agreed.

"Then do tell him, do. There's a dear. He likes you, you know. Oh, my, yes. I've seen him looking at you. And he's more and more daggers at Bill. Surely you realize . . . if you tell him, explain he must allow Ellen more rest, but at the same time, more normal activity, why then, dear . . ."

Jan went to the dresser. She brushed her short shining curls, and made up her face. Mrs. Mayor had said she looked pale.

But she must not look pale. She must not look frightened. Above all, no matter what, she must not show her loathing of Ian.

Mrs. Mayor said anxiously, "He's concerned, dear. You will be right down?"

Jan turned. "Mrs. Mayor, are you afraid of Ian?

Mrs. Mayor's plump face seemed to shrivel. "Afraid! Afraid? I?" The words were supposed to express denial. The tone expressed affirmation. She went on, "But he is odd, you see. I just asked him if he'd found help in Mercer for Vera, and can you imagine? He gave me such a look! I thought . . . why, Jan, dear, I only wanted . . . surely he understood. He just shook his head, but those eyes of his . . . It was just my imagination, of course. But still . . . you will hurry, won't you, dear?"

Jan smoothed the red dress at her hips.

She had chosen it that morning in a burst of . . .

what had it been? Bravado? Courage? She drew a long slow breath. Either one, she felt unprepared to see Ian and Bill.

She didn't know what to do.

Mrs. Ballantine? Or was it Sarah Jarvis . . .

Ellen . . . .

The black coil rising from the white cushion . . .

She told herself that she must wait, see. She dare not endanger the old woman who was at Ian's mercy. She dare not endanger Ellen . . .

And for David's sake she must know the truth.

"Ready?" Mrs. Mayor asked, twisting her fat hands in her blue cotton dress, and at Jan's nod, went ahead, bouncing into the hall, then down the steps, crying, "Here she is. No ill effects at all. You see . . . I did tell you, Ian. Jan is too hardy to be frightened." She turned to smile at Jan, "Even of snakes, dear."

Ian ignored Mrs. Mayor, turned blue flame eyes on Jan. "You mustn't let Ballantine Lodge get you."

She swallowed the metallic taste of fear, the sour taste of loathing. She said, "I've forgotten about last night."

"Good." He looked as if he were going to say something else.

But Jan cut in, "I thought Ellen might have come down, Ian."

"I'm afraid she's the same. I realize this is difficult for you, Jan. But . . ."

Again she cut in. "Ian, you must listen to me. If Ellen goes on like this much longer, you'll have to do something more for her. She must have a doctor. You're taking chances with her . . . her sanity, possibly even her life. Chances you have no business taking."

"You know very little about it, Jan. Not that I don't appreciate your concern, believe me. And you can't imagine how sorry Ellen is that she finds it so difficult to see you. She knows you want to finish your business here and get away. And of course, if you like, as I once suggested before, I could have her sign whatever documents are involved, then . . ."

"But we aren't talking about that now," Jan said briskly. "We are talking about Ellen's life."

"That's all a part of it, Jan."

"Then I must wait. There are many questions that Ellen, and only Ellen, can answer. Time isn't important, my father always said, it's getting the job done right."

"Your father?" Ian's craggy face seemed suddenly set in cement. "Yes, that does sound like him."

The raw bitterness in Ian's voice seemed to sear Jan. Ian had not only known her father years before, but obviously had hated him. Why?

Had this hatred extended to David as well?

Did it extend to Jan herself?

But Ian was smiling at her indulgently. "Shall I ask Mrs. Mayor to prepare us a before luncheon drink?"

The superficial quiet of the long day had been in odd contrast to Jan's tumultuous thoughts.

As she went to bed that night, she looked ahead, dreading the morning to come.

Ian's blue flame eyes . . .

Bill's dark ones . . .

Both watching her, watching her as if she, she herself, held the last piece on a chess board, the last that could move.

She must do something. She must do something quickly. Quickly, quickly . . . With those words, she drifted into sleep.

There was a terrible pounding at the door. A pounding that finally broke through the shelter of her troubled dreams.

Wakening, wrapped in chill, she cried, "Yes, yes. I'm coming," and grabbed a robe, and raced to open the door.

Chapter 14

WHATEVER HAD happened was bad, Jan knew.

A single glance told her that much, although it told her no more.

Vera stood there, trembling. Her young face was gray with horror, and wet with tears. Her white uniform was wrinkled.

"Oh, please," she cried. "Help me. Help me. I'm so afraid," and collapsed into Jan's arms.

"Mrs. Ballantine?" Jan demanded, her heart sinking, already knowing the answer, already certain.

"Oh, yes, yes. But please, do something. Call a doctor. We need a doctor. Jan, do something for her."

Jan pushed Vera's clinging body away, and ran down the hall into the dim room. She went down on her knees beside the pillow-stacked bed.

Mrs. Ballantine's tiny waxen face had wrinkled into a lifeless mask. Her hazel eyes were firmly closed. Her sunken lips were sealed.

Jan, remembering the few words Mrs. Ballantine had spoken, knew that the old lady had said the last she would ever say, would never speak again, and Jan bowed her head and wept.

Vera, clinging to the door cried, "I couldn't help it. I was just having a little nap. He said I could. She was all right before I lay down. I looked at her. I really did. I watched her all the time, just like he told me to." The quick, frightened words suddenly faded into a meaningless whimper.

Jan raised her head to look.

Ian had come in. He wore a pale green robe, and dark trousers, and his red-gold head gleamed in the lamp light. He said in a low hard voice, "What is it now?"

116

Without waiting for an answer, he came to stand beside Jan, and looked down at Mrs. Ballantine. He remained that way, head bent, still, for a long moment. Then he sighed, and touched her shriveled arm gently.

"I suppose she's had another stroke, a last one. It was something I knew could happen at any time. Still . . . still . . ." He sighed again. He leaned closer, carefully pulled the coverlet over the small, empty face, and as he did, his shadow fell over it.

It was as if a momentary expression had rippled across Mrs. Ballantine's face, as if she had cringed at his touch.

Jan shuddered, wiped tears from her burning eyes.

Ian asked, "Would you see to Vera, Jan? There are things I have to do, and now."

He went out, treading softly.

As he went by her, Vera made a smothered whimpering sound.

Jan went to her, put a hand on her arm, and saw, past Vera's shoulder, that Ellen had awakened. She was standing near the steps, clinging to the bannister. Her golden hair flowed over her shoulders, her haggard face was white, twisted. Her loose silken robe was an iridescent gray. From that distance, in that distorted light, she looked like a single quivering tear drop.

She whispered, "What's wrong, Ian? What's the matter, Ian?"

Jan couldn't hear Ian's answer.

But Ellen cried, "Tell me. I want to know. I don't want to sleep now. Tell me what's wrong."

Ian put a big arm around her shoulders, again said something that Jan couldn't hear. She couldn't hear his answer then, and what happened came so quickly that she couldn't even move.

For Ellen turned on him. She turned wildly inside his arm, and pounded his chest with small fists, and screamed, "No, no, no!"

Ian seemed to freeze. He stood there, towering over her, and let her hit him, once, twice, three times. And then, as Vera cried out, he swept Ellen up, enfolded her in his arms, her face against his chest, her struggling body imprisoned, and carried her, the iridescent robe trailing light behind them, down the hallway and out of sight.

But not out of hearing. Her screams seemed to echo back to the others for a long time. They echoed back until a door closed sharply, and the hall was still.

Vera sobbed, "I want my mother. I want to go home."

"I'll send you home," Jan promised softly. "You'll be home soon."

And hearing herself say those words, she wondered when she would be going home, when she would leave Ballantine Lodge forever.

Bill, standing near the stairs, gave her one long sober questioning look before he turned and went downstairs.

She didn't know how long he had been there. She didn't know what he had heard. She didn't know where he was going. But she wished that he had stayed with her.

There was no time to think then.

Mrs. Mayor, for once speechless, came and led Vera away.

Jan went downstairs.

Bill was just putting down the telephone.

She looked at him, small, vulnerable and very frightened.

"The doctor's on his way."

"But he can't do anything, can he?"

Bill gave her a sharp look. "No. Of course not." He glanced sideways at the stairs, plainly looking for Ian.

"I don't understand," she said faintly.

"Don't understand what?"

"But why did she die? Why now?"

Bill didn't answer her.

Within a few moments, Ian came down. He looked calm, unruffled. If he was grieving, it didn't show on his craggy face, in his blue flame eyes.

"Ellen?" Jan asked.

"She'll be all right."

Bill told Ian that the doctor had said he would come right out from Mercer.

Ian nodded, thanked him for making the call.

They waited for what seemed to be a long time.

When the doctor came at last, he was so very old, so very stout, that Jan wondered how he had managed to climb the terrace steps.

Ian took him up to Mrs. Ballantine's room.

They were there for a few minutes.

Jan waited, breath held, until they returned.

When they did, the doctor sat down at the table, drew a pen from his jacket and began, with a trembling hand to fill out a form, struggling all the while to swallow a series of body-shaking yawns.

Jan tried, once, to suggest he check on Ellen. But Ian gave her a hard blue look, and the words died on her lips.

The doctor made a few phone calls when he had finished the forms. Then, still yawning, he departed.

Within the hour, an ambulance arrived. Ian let two burly men into the house. He led them up to the second floor. They carried between them a basket-like thing, long, narrow, wrapped in a dark green sheet. When they came down, it seemed no heavier than before, though Jan knew they were carrying then all that was left of Mrs. Ballantine, taking her away forever.

Tears filled Jan's eyes.

The old lady had spoken to her, said a few incoherent words, and that same night she died.

She had spoken, and she had died.

Why? Why?

Jan swallowed hard, asked in a thin voice, "I suppose they do an autopsy?"

"An autopsy?" Ian repeated. "What for? At her age, in her condition . . ."

"It seems so sudden," Jan said weakly.

"It always does," Bill told her.

She wondered if there were a warning in his words.

"My mother is at peace now," Ian said gently.

Jan looked down at her clenched fists, hoping to hide the wave of sickness that swept her at his effrontery. The old lady that she still thought of as Mrs. Ballantine was not Mrs. Ballantine, was not Ian's mother. She had been Sarah Jarvis.

She had said a few words, and died.

Death was in the house. It was in the house now, and had been there before. Or did it have another name? Was its true name murder?

Murder . . .

How had Thalia really died . . .

How had Sarah Jarvis . . .

Jan asked herself suddenly if Ian could have known that the old lady had managed to speak a few words to Jan.

And he said, "The Ballantine curse," and sighed.

Dawn and daylight seemed a long time in coming.

Jan remembered the pink glow that had shone in the east the morning eight days before when she climbed down from the train that brought her to Mercer. She remembered her eagerness to see Ellen, and Ian Ballantine. To see them, to understand, to know the truth. To know, at last, why David died yearning for the wife who didn't come to him.

It seemed, then, a simple thing.

She supposed she would see and know.

She would help Ellen.

Now Jan knew that what had seemed simple was swathed in complexities. The truth she had sought was buried somewhere within sinister purpose that she had barely glimpsed.

Ellen was sleeping, Ian said calmly, sipping his coffee, and looking into Jan's eyes.

The three of them, Bill, Ian, and Jan, were at the table. For Mrs. Mayor, averting her red and swollen face, had insisted that everyone sit down to eat. "It's the only way you can keep your strength," she told them.

Jan swallowed and looked down at her eggs. She didn't want them. She wasn't hungry.

When she looked up, Ellen was in the doorway.

She wavered there for a moment, then came gliding in, gliding, with her robe trailing her, like a sleepwalker.

Her blue eyes, blood-shot and full of anguish were fixed on Ian. "I couldn't be alone," she whispered.

"You'll only upset yourself more," he told her.

He got up, went to meet her.

Jan said quickly, "Will you have some coffee, Ellen?"

But Ellen didn't answer. Her eyes were still fixed on Ian, her golden head tipped back now. "When will it be? The funeral? When, Ian?"

He said quietly, "There will be services this afternoon. Just as she would want it." He paused. "She'll be cremated, Ellen. And I will be with her. *I* will be with her."

Ellen gasped, "No!" and her legs seemed to melt from under her. She crumpled into Ian's arms, sobbing, "Sarah. Oh, I want Sarah."

Ian, holding her, looked past her golden head at Jan and Bill. "Just like when she was a child," he said. "It's always been that way. When she was hurt, she cried for Sarah Jarvis. She always cried for Sarah, instead of our mother."

The room seemed full of breathless silence as he carried Ellen away.

Ellen always cried for Sarah Jarvis, Ian had said.

Jan, loathing him, admired his resourcefulness.

For she knew that Ellen had meant something quite different. Ellen had been protesting Sarah's death, cremation.

Ellen's few words had been all the confirmation that Jan needed for certainty.

The old lady taken away forever just a little while earlier was Sarah Jarvis.

She managed to speak a few words.

That night she died.

She died, while Vera was napping.

Jan looked at Bill, "What are we going to do?"

Before he could answer her, Ian returned. Without a word, he sat down, refilled his coffee cup.

Jan said, "I'll go to the services with you, Ian."

He glanced at her, then away. "Thank you for offering to, but it will be very simple, very private. My mother would have preferred it that way."

Jan choked back an angry retort. She didn't let herself shout that maybe his mother would have, but what about Sarah Jarvis?

Jan pushed back her chair, nodded at Bill, and went upstairs. Her door was half open. She paused, her heart suddenly beating hard, remembering the black coil rising to strike her. She was afraid to go into her room, afraid of what she would find there.

Then she heard a long-drawn breath, a sob. She thrust the door in.

Vera peered at her from behind a crumpled handkerchief. "He told me to stay in there, in that room, but I couldn't," she mumbled. "And I didn't want to go down, not until Bill's ready to drive me in to Mercer. I just . . ."

"It's okay," Jan reassured her. "Are you all ready now?"

Vera nodded.

"Then it won't be long, and you'll be home again. You can forget all this."

"But nothing . . . I never saw anybody die before, Jan" Vera shuddered. "And it isn't my fault. Honest, it isn't. It was just . . . well, I was taking a nap. He said I could do that."

Jan remembered the wrinkled white nylon uniform, the sleep-pale face, the tousled sandy hair. It had been a long nap, a deep one, she thought. And saw Ian, no more than a big dark shadow in the night, head bent to listen at the door. She saw him easing the door open, crossing the room in long silent strides. She saw him bending over the tiny still form on the bed . . . and then?

"It wasn't my fault," Vera was saying insistently.

"Nobody blames you, Vera. She was an old woman, a sick one . . ."

"But did you see how he looked me in the face? Did you see it? And, Jan, honest, I told him just last night, just hours before it happened . . . I told him I thought he ought to have a doctor in. I told him I thought she could be helped some. I know it's crazy, but I just had the feeling she could talk if she wanted to. That she wasn't nearly as bad off as she seemed, and you know what he said?" Vera added spitefully, "He said I was imagining things. But, Jan, if he'd had a doctor in then . . ."

Jan demanded, "You told him you thought she could talk?"

Vera nodded, her tearful eyes wide.

Jan felt her throat tighten. She turned away from Vera. She stared at the distant eastern horizon. Ian had known from what Vera told him that Sarah Jarvis had been trying to speak.

Jan could see him bending over the still form on the bed. And then . . . ? There had been no mark on Sarah. The doctor, someone else, would have seen anything obvious. What had Ian done as he leaned over the pillow-stacked bed? And then Jan saw him reach for a pillow, press it carefully over the small waxen face, the drug-clouded hazel eyes closed, the shrunken lips sealed forever.

Whispering, Jan asked, "Did you mention I'd been in the room with her before, Vera?" and held her breath.

"Of course I didn't." Vera cried. "How could I? It would only have meant another bawling out. And anyway, what difference does it make! He's the one that's crazy, not me. I told him . . ." and Jan breathed again.

A little later, Mrs. Mayor came to say that Ian was waiting to drive Vera in to Mercer.

The young girl protested, "But Bill said he would."

Mrs. Mayor shrugged plump shoulders. "Ian has to go in anyway, you know."

"But I don't want to go with him," Vera cried.

"Tell him, not me," Mrs. Mayor answered. "I don't run this house, Vera. Now be a good girl, and come along. He's waiting for you. And there's been enough trouble so don't you make more."

Vera's protests grew weaker and weaker as Jan and Mrs. Mayor helped her take her things downstairs, and when she saw Ian, she said, red swollen eyes lowered, voice a whisper, "I'm sorry it happened."

He answered gently, "Never mind. It wasn't your fault. We all know that," but his blue flame eyes flicked sideways at Jan.

Chapter 15

SHE WATCHED from the terrace until the black limousine had disappeared beyond the furthest curve, until its trail of floating pink dust had settled.

Ian had told Vera to stay in the room at the end of the hall. He had arranged to drive her to Mercer. He would put her on a bus, and she, like Sarah Jarvis, would be gone forever from Ballantine Lodge.

Vera had told Ian that she thought Sarah could speak.

And both Vera and Sarah were beyond Jan's reach, her questions.

She shivered as she went into the house.

Mrs Mayor was clearing the table. "It's terrible," she said. "I just can't believe it. Why, I would have thought Mrs. Ballantine could have gone on forever, little as she was, sick as she was. She wouldn't let go, Jan. You could feel it. The fight in her. She held on so strong."

Jan, remembering the drug-clouded hazel eyes, nodded. She, too, had sensed the struggle in the old woman.

"And to be taken off, cremated, put away all alone," Mrs. Mayor sighed. "I don't know what he's thinking of. It's not right, Jan."

Jan nodded again.

Mrs. Mayor sighed. "Well, there's always work to do, and that's a blessing. In times like these, yes, work's a blessing." She took the loaded tray into plump hands and bounced out of the room, trailing words that Jan didn't listen to.

She returned to the terrace. She passed by the white leatherette chair, and sat in one closer to the red stone wall. The whispering silence seemed to settle heavily around her.

The sun turned the waist-high pampas grass on the meadows below to silver, and made streaks of fire on the mountain's red ridges, and spread thick sweet heat upon the terrace.

But Jan, thinking of Sarah, felt a chill, a chill like the touch of death enfold her.

Sarah had died because she had spoken. Ian knew that. He knew that she might, some time, somehow, speak to Jan. He didn't know that she had already spoken to Jan. He had killed her to prevent that. Jan asked herself what Sarah had known that had forced Ian, after so long, to silence her? What had Sarah said?

Sarah had been with the family in Rome, and met David. She said, "David . . ." She said, "Both beautiful. One of love. One of stone." She said, "No. Thalia."

One love. One stone.

Why did Sarah mention Thalia then? Why did she say, "No. Thalia."

Jan remembered what she had thought of before. One with a heart of love. One with a heart of stone.

Ellen had loved David, married him.

But Thalia . . . Thalia had looked adoringly at David. Thalia had loved him.

But Ellen had loved him, too. Ellen, wearing widow's mourning, was not feigning her sorrow at his death.

What had Sarah Jarvis been trying to say? What did Ian fear she could say?

Jan thought of the first time she had seen Ellen.

She came up the red stone steps, with Bill right at her heels. She froze at the edge of the terrace, unable to move. Ellen was there, golden hair floating on her black-clad shoulders, her face twisted with grief, her thin arms reaching out, while Jan thought, But that's not Ellen. That can't be Ellen, echoing her heart's disbelief.

In the doorway, Ian stood like a great golden god out of an ancient myth. He stood there, prolonging the moment in which Ellen wept, sobbed David's name, in Jan's arms.

He had wanted that moment prolonged.

He had wanted Jan to know, be overwhelmed by, Ellen's sorrow.

Ellen's sorrow . . .

But was it Ellen's sorrow? she asked herself.

Or was it Thalia's?

Who was the girl in the room upstairs now?

Who wept, and whispered David's name, and cried for Sarah?

A few more small pieces fell into place. The pattern sharpened beneath the thinning shadow of Mercer Mountain.

Jan shivered in the hot sunlight, and buried her head in her hands.

Was it Thalia who had flung herself to the red ridges below, and to her death?

Or was it Ellen?

Had Sarah been trying to tell Jan that Ellen was dead?

Ian was anxious that Jan finish her business with Ellen, yet hardly allowed her to spend any time with the girl. He concealed his eagerness that Jan leave Ballantine Lodge behind a superficial charm that was a sign of vanity strong enough to blind him to her response to him. Was that same vanity a sign of the kind of arrogance which could lead to murder? Would it lead to murder again?

Briefly, Jan wondered if when she had come to Ballantine Lodge she had been touched by some infectious madness that lingered in the house. Had she crossed the invisible line between sense and sanity? Had the weight of those suspicions she brought with her finally crushed her into this quicksand of horror?

She allowed herself to face those doubts, to wish, almost hopefully, that they were fact, that everything that had happened in Ballantine Lodge had been nothing more than a nightmare from which she would soon awaken.

But then she swept her doubts away. They were no nightmare. She would not awaken.

She straightened up, looked again across the sprawling meadows to the eastern horizon. Earlier she had said to

Bill, "What will we do?" He hadn't answered her, for Ian came into the room then.

What would Bill have said?

Jan knew the answer. He would have looked at her with sober dark eyes, told her to leave Ballantine Lodge.

But she couldn't. She wouldn't. She had to know the truth. For David. For Sarah. For Ellen.

Jan forced herself to her feet. She went from the hot sunlight that didn't warm her into the cool whispering silence of the house.

The door was closed.

The room was very still.

She knocked. There was no answer.

She tried the knob. The door swung open.

A blaze of light struck her eyes.

Every lamp in the sun-filled room was alight and glowing.

Ellen lay on a green lounge before the big green-draped window. She turned and looked at Jan, anguished eyes widening.

Jan said quickly, going to stand beside her, "I came to see if you wanted anything, Ellen."

The girl shook her golden head. "I loved her, you know. I wouldn't have let anything happen to her, not ever, ever. And now, right now, I guess, she's been. . . ." Ellen covered her face with thin hands. "Where's Ian?"

"In town. He took Vera . . ."

"Yes. Then it's now, isn't it? There's nobody left for me. She's gone . . . and . . ."

"You mean Sarah, don't you?" Jan asked softly.

"Sarah? Sarah?" Ellen's haggard face turned red, then paled. Her mouth twisted. Then she flung herself sideways on the lounge, her body trembling. "No," she screamed. "No. You're mixing me up. Nothing happened. He just sent her away. So there's nobody left for me."

Jan said, "Yes. Yes, Ellen, I understand. But you're not alone. You have your brothers. You have Ian, and Carl, and soon . . ."

"Carl? Carl?" Ellen whispered.

Jan leaned forward. "I know he's at school. But one of these days . . ."

Ellen made a sound, a strangled sound that was part sob, part laughter.

"Lie back and rest, and think of good things," Jan said quickly. She carefully tucked the green robe around Ellen's body, and as she did, she felt Ellen tremble, withdraw from her touch.

"Good things," Ellen said bitterly. She lay back, her ravaged face averted. "What good things? I don't remember any."

"There was that time with David," Jan said softly. "Remember that."

"David . . . yes, David. I loved him. I would have saved him if I could. I would have gone to him if I could, Jan."

"He was coming to you, Ellen. He was packed, waiting only for a plane reservation, when he got sick. He was coming to you because of the letters you wrote him. The last things he said, his last words, were about you. He loved you. He asked me to come to you, to help you . . ."

Ellen was staring, her wide blue eyes overflowing with tears, past Jan, staring at the door. "Ian," she whispered. "Ian."

Jan turned, her heart giving a quick leap of fright. But the door was closed still. Ian hadn't come in.

"He's in town," she told Ellen. "Remember? I told you he took Vera to Mercer."

But Ellen's eyes remained fixed on the door. She whispered, "I didn't write to David. I wouldn't have. I wanted to save him, I tell you. I would have . . . if I could have I would have saved him. I would have gone to him. . . ."

"Think of the good days," Jan said quickly. "The good days with David in Beirut."

"In Beirut? No, no, it was Rome," Ellen cried.

And Jan knew. She was sure.

The girl who trembled on the lounge, her blue eyes wild now, was not the girl that David had married. The girl that David had married had fallen to her death on the rocks below Ballantine Lodge.

"That was in Rome. The only good days. Sarah . . . David . . . my dreams . . . the only good days, before my dreams went wrong."

Before her dreams went wrong . . .

David had said that he met Thalia first. Then he had met Ellen and loved her.

Thalia . . . with her heart of love.

Ellen . . . with her heart of stone.

That was what Sarah Jarvis had been trying to tell Jan, she knew.

And Bill?

He had said that he had known Ellen slightly in Beirut. He had said that she was changed now. Had he been deceived? Or had he known the truth all along? Was he here to find out what had happened to the real Ellen? Or was he here to protect that girl who was now pretending to be Ellen.

Jan said softly, "In Rome, when you, and Thalia, and Sarah, were all traveling with Ian and Carl, and you met David, something happened, didn't it?"

Ellen's eyes remained fixed on the door. She didn't answer.

"You married David, and you went to Beirut. And you stayed there, and were happy, weren't you? Until you had to come home."

"Thalia. Thalia was ill," Ellen said hoarsely. "Ian said I had to. So I did. I did what he said."

"And then . . . after you were here for a while?"

Ellen writhed on the lounge, threw her head from side to side so that her golden hair became a golden veil, hiding her face. She screamed, "Nothing happened, I tell you. Go away. Go away from here. No one can help me. No one. But believe me, I didn't write any letters to David. I didn't. Just go away and forget us. Forget us, Jan." The words became incoherent sobs, heart-rending sobs that filled the light-blazing room.

Jan touched Ellen's shoulder, whispered, "It's going

to be all right," and went out, closing the door softly behind her.

She walked on quiet feet down the corridor through the whispering silence whose words she could now understand.

Ellen had come back to Ballantine Lodge from Beirut, and written those pleading letters to David. Somehow she had died. Thalia had been terrorized into taking Ellen's place. Sarah had been terrorized, then drugged, so that the substitution would not be revealed when Jan herself arrived.

And Ian, beneath the red-gold charm of an ancient god, was himself the breathing epitome of the Mercer Monster.

Greed.

The Mercer Monster, a thing of splintering wood, a weathered log, decorated with rusty nails, bits of brass, tin cans. A thing of no heart, of no soul. An empty monument to the greed of man.

The Ballantine curse . . .

Ian, playing an evil game, in which only he knew the rules, using everyone around him, Sarah, Ellen, Thalia, and Carl, but where was Carl really? as pawns on puppet strings, while he plotted to gain the half of the Olney fortune that had been David's.

Or would he be satisfied with that?

Did he want more?

Jan shivered, remembering how his blue flame eyes looked at her.

Ian balked, or threatened, had turned to murder once, perhaps even twice.

She had to protect herself, to protect the girl that she had always known as Ellen.

Jan told herself that she had to do something. But what? How could she unmask Ian?

She hesitated at her room, then opened the door.

She froze on the threshold.

A tall silhouette, shadow dark, blocked the sun at the window.

Chapter 16

FOR A SINGLE, dreading moment, she thought that Ian awaited her.

Then the silhouette turned, became Bill. He said, "Come in, Jan. Why are you standing there? I have to talk to you."

She drew a long slow breath, relieved that she didn't have to face Ian yet, that she would still have time to think, plan, more than anything, to collect her scattered thoughts.

But there was Bill, leaning against the blue-draped window, high cheekbones showing in his drawn face, beaked nose predatory, dark eyes shuttered. Bill, with the hunter look, watching her.

She drew another long slow breath, and went into the room. She closed the door softly behind her, and went to sit on the bed.

Bill turned sideways, gave a quick slanting look out, then turned back to her. "Where were you? I had hoped you had sense enough to leave. Now. Before Ian gets back."

It was what she wanted to do with all her heart. But she ran her hand wearily through her black curls. She shook her head wearily. "I can't, Bill. Not yet."

"There's an old saying. 'Discretion is the better part of valor'. Do you remember ever having been impressed by it?"

"Not very much."

He shot another glance out of the window.

She supposed he was watching for Ian.

She asked, "Is that what you wanted to talk about?"

"Yes. And you ought to have been impressed by discretion. It makes all the difference at the moment."

"There are enough riddles around here, Bill."

"Don't you remember that snake, Jan?"

"I remember it." She paused, then added softly, "And those two men, carrying Sarah Jarvis out . . ."

"Sarah Jarvis."

She went on, "And Ellen. And Thalia. And Carl."

Bill said, "Thalia is dead, Jan. And Carl . . . there is no Carl. He was a boy, a part-time actor, down on his luck in Rome, wanting fare to get back to the States. He was hired to play a part. He played it and came home."

She looked into Bill's face. "You've known that all the time. You've known the whole thing."

"I found out about Carl a couple of days ago."

"How?"

"By checking around." Then, "Jan, why won't you believe me, trust me? You must leave now."

"Why should I?" she demanded. "I don't know you. Or anything about you. And what I do know . . ."

"What you do know . . ." he prompted her, his voice deep, hard. She didn't answer him.

He crossed to her in three long, easy strides. He stood over her. "Well?"

"You said you knew David and Ellen in Beirut. If you did, then you lied to me. Then you made yourself part of it. If you ever knew Ellen, you must know that the girl Ian calls Ellen is not the girl David brought to Beirut from Rome. She is not. I'm certain that she's Thalia. The real Ellen is dead." She paused. Bill didn't say anything. She went on, "If you didn't recognize the substitution, then you never knew Ellen, or David. Then . . ."

Bill cut in, "I did, Jan."

"Why didn't you tell me?"

"I wanted you to settle the estate quickly, to leave quickly.

"But why?" Again, he didn't answer her. She said, "I've seen you looking at her, Bill. I know how you feel about her."

"I pity her."

"Pity her, Bill? Isn't it more than that? Aren't you in

love with her? Or is it the money she was to have? Are you, like Ian . . ."

"I am not Ian," Bill told her. Then, more gently, "There is such a thing as a point of no return, Jan. We're there now." His hand dropped to her shoulder. "You must trust me, Jan. Leave Ballantine Lodge while you can."

"How can I trust you? Why should I?"

He drew her to her feet. His arms came around her.

She wanted to pull away, but the sweet electricity of his touch held her. She reminded herself that she was Jan Olney. She was twenty-three years old. She could take care of herself. She always had and she always would. She could almost hear her father's voice telling her that when she was a child, frightened at being sent away to school, frightened at being alone for the first time. She reminded herself of who she was, of that self-sufficiency of which she had always been so proud, of which Bill had seemed to disapprove so strongly. She reminded herself it was supposed to support her now. But that didn't help. She didn't want to be alone any more. She needed someone to lean on. She needed Bill.

She let herself lean against him.

He touched her cheek. His long mouth turned down in a grin of sudden awareness. "Do you remember the night of the snake, Jan?"

"Please stop talking about that," she whispered.

"I'm glad to see that you're part feminine anyway."

"Thank you. On the day I arrived you called me a canary. You've told me I'm hard-headed, stubborn, and stupid, by implication. Now you tell me I'm only part feminine."

"Are you keeping track? I wonder why."

She didn't know why herself. She didn't answer him. He bent his head slowly, and pressed his lips to hers.

For a little while that seemed forever there was no terror, no time. There was only a sweet singing joy in her.

Then he raised his head. "That's one reason why."

"Why what?" she asked breathlessly.

"Why you should trust me."

She was suddenly cold, cold within the circle of his arms. She drew away from him.

His face changed. His grin was gone. The gentleness had gone out of his voice when he said, "So be it." He went to the closet, jerked down her suitcase. "Start packing, Jan."

"I can't. I have to know what happened to David's wife."

"Is that the only reason why? Haven't you been think-of revenge, Jan? Revenge for David?"

She gasped, "What do you mean? I came thinking that Ellen needed my help."

"And that's why you've stalled in settling David's estate? That's the only reason why?"

"What did you mean about David?" she demanded.

"No. Don't let me put the idea into your mind. I checked it out, Jan. David did die of the fever he seemed to. He picked it up first in Alexandria. It came back on him, just as they told you in Beirut."

"You thought that David might have been murdered," she whispered. "You checked it out. Ian knew my father, and hated him, Bill. Is that what made you wonder about David's death?"

Bill nodded.

"Ellen came home, and wrote those letters to David . . ."

"What letters?"

"Asking him to come to her, begging him, saying she was afraid. She wrote them before . . . it was before Thalia died, Bill."

"That was the important something I didn't know," Bill said harshly. He touched her shoulder, turned her to the closet. "Hurry. Pack now."

And from below, they heard the sound of a car.

Bill swore under his breath. "That's Ian. Listen to me, Jan. No matter what happens, don't let Ellen sign those papers. Not while you're here. Do you understand me? Her signature is your death warrant. And hers. You can't die first. But you will have to die afterwards. I'm sure now. I'm sure. Find some excuse to leave. I'll see

you make it. Now . . . yes . . . Jan, go down to him now.
Stall him for a little while."

She tried to say something, to protest, but Bill caught
her to him briefly, and suddenly, without knowing how
she had gotten there, she was in the hall, and Bill was
saying, "Stall him, Jan."

She nodded, brushed her dark curls. She ran until she
reached the foyer, and then, slowing down, forcing a
smile to her lips, she went out to the terrace.

Ian was just coming up the steps, the sun bright on his
red-gold hair. He gave her a weary smile, and she smiled
back at him, consciously deepening her dimples, and
hoping that what she felt, her loathing, her horror of
him didn't show on her face.

"It's good to see you waiting here for me like this," he
said. "I wish you could always be."

She knew that his blue flame eyes were searching her
face. She knew that she should answer him. But she
could think of nothing to say.

He sat down on the white leatherette chair, and
leaned back, and loosened his tie.

She thought of the black coil, the snake, he had left
there, rising to strike at her. The snake, its venom drawn,
meant only to frighten her enough so that she would
leave Ballantine Lodge.

He jerked a chair closer to his, gestured at it. "Come
here, Jan."

She went to him. She went to sit beside him, fearful,
dreading his nearness.

He said, "Do you remember, Jan? I told you once,
when talking about David and Ellen, that I believe in
love at first sight? That I believe in love?"

She nodded slowly, knowing that she was right. He
was after all the Olney fortune. And the black coil
rising from the chair? Not to drive her away. Not quite.
Only to frighten her into settling David's estate. Then,
Ian had planned to woo her, sure that he could keep
her in Ballantine Lodge until . . .

He was saying, "Perhaps this isn't the best time, but I
want you to be thinking of me, Jan. To be thinking of me,

not as your brother-in-law, but as a man. As a man who needs you and wants you." He reached out, took her hand.

At his touch, a wave of dizziness swept her. Fear became breathtaking pain in her throat. His fingers closed around hers, imprisoning them. A shudder moved through her. She knew that he saw it, felt it. His face changed, hardened, his blue flame eyes slid away from hers. His hand tightened on her fingers.

"But perhaps it is too soon," he said softly. "There's time, Jan." Then, "Or is there also someone else."

"Someone else?" She managed the two words in a hoarse whisper.

He chuckled. "Bill, perhaps? But then, he'll be leaving today, you know. A house bereaved such as this one is no place for a guest. Particularly not an unwelcome guest."

She swallowed against the breathtaking pain that was fear. She moved her hands in his.

He reluctantly let it go. "I do not like to be inhospitable, but I see no reason to encourage a rival."

She said finally, "Bill isn't your rival, Ian. It's just that . . ."

"It's too soon for you to know how you feel about me?" Ian asked. "Never mind, Jan, dear. Bill had long since completed his business with Ellen anyway. I thought he would be good for her, but . . ." Ian's massive shoulders moved in a shrug. ". . . but my poor sister . . ." He paused, shot a quick blue look at Jan. "Have you seen her?"

Jan knew that Ellen would tell him about her earlier visit. She said, "I stopped in to see how she was."

"Oh did you?" Ian said softly, rising to his feet. "And?"

"She's very upset, Ian. I do think you ought to have the doctor."

"Perhaps I will," he said smoothly. "And now . . . if you'll excuse me for a few minutes . . ."

She nodded in wordless relief.

Whatever Bill had planned must be done by now, she thought.

Ian said, in a voice that made it an order, "Wait for me here, Jan, please," and went indoors.

It was only then that she realized that she had not told Ian she was leaving. She had not found an excuse that would serve. And if he were determined to have the whole Olney fortune, he would never let her go. Never.

The real Ellen was dead.

Sarah was dead.

Jan asked herself if she was to be next.

And what of the girl upstairs? The girl who called herself Ellen now? Would Ian allow her to live? Would he dare allow her to live?

Jan waited on the terrace.

She waited, not for Ian, but for Bill.

She stared across the rippling waves of pampas grass that spread to the eastern horizon, and thought of her home, her friends, and wondered if she would ever see them again.

Chapter 17

BUT. BILL didn't come.

She wondered uneasily where he was, what he was doing.

She thought that if she were entrapped in a dream terror would have drawn her out of sleep and into the safety of awakening. But since it was no dream, there was no wakening safety to be drawn to.

The bright sun still layered the rippling pampas grass with silver. The blue arc of the sky spread peacefully from the mountain range to the edge of the great sprawling meadow. Within the house, there was the clink of dishes, the thud of footsteps.

The sight and sound of normalcy surrounded her, the false calm of Ballantine Lodge.

Ian had gone indoors. He would be upstairs now. Upstairs in the lamp-blazing room. He would be talking to, questioning, the girl Jan had known only as Ellen, could think of only as Ellen.

Jan wondered how much of her conversation with Ellen the girl would remember, repeat. How much she would say to Ian, and what he would make of it.

David, dying had whispered, *What's happening to Ellen?*

Why doesn't she come?

What's wrong with her?

What do her letters mean, Jan?

She had promised him that she would find out. She would go to Ellen. She would answer the summons for help that David could not answer himself, would never be able to answer himself.

Ellen had written those letters.

The Ellen that David had married . . .

138

She had wanted David to come to her, pleaded that he come to her . . .

And then she had died.

The girl upstairs? The girl who called herself Ellen now?

A cold rippling shiver swept through Jan.

She could hear the quick denial, "I didn't write to David. I wouldn't have. I wanted to save him. I would have saved him if I could. I loved him."

There was too much honesty, too much conviction in those words. Jan had to believe them. Yet she didn't really know what they meant.

Would Ian know?

Would the distraught girl in the light-blazing room tell him that Jan had asked about the letters?

Would he know then that Jan realized Ellen was dead?

Would he know then that Jan realized Thalia had taken her place?

Bill had said that once the documents were signed her death warrant, and Jan's, too, would have been signed. Jan could not die first, but she must die afterwards.

But if Ian wanted all the Olney fortune, Jan could not die yet.

There was still time.

But only if she were able to deceive Ian into believing that there was a chance for him.

Only if he had not sensed her withdrawal, the shudder that went through her, when he took her hand.

She straightened in her chair.

She must smile at him, deepen her dimples, hope that in his arrogance he would deceive himself well enough so that she could deceive him.

That way she could make time.

She shivered, and looked with unbelieving eyes into the peaceful white sunlight. It seemed impossible that she should sit under such a peaceful sun, listening to the home-like sounds from within the house, while she sought invisible escape from the trap in which she waited.

The home-like sounds came closer. Mrs. Mayor bustled out to the terrace, carrying a loaded tray. "Oh, there you are, dear," she cried. "I was wondering. Yes, I was. The house does seem so still, my, yes. In he came. 'Make tea', he says. And up he went. To see Ellen, of course. Poor child. To tell her it's over, I expect. 'Over and done.' That's what he always says when something bad happens. 'Over and done.' " Mrs. Mayor took a deep, quick breath. Then, "You're quiet, too. Jan, dear, I know you're thinking of that poor old woman. Of Mrs. Ballantine. But still, that's how it goes, isn't it?"

Jan nodded.

"Now, dear, you aren't planning to run away and leave us, are you?" Mrs. Mayor adjusted dishes, linens, stood back to survey her handiwork. "Poor Ellen . . . it would be so awful for her to be alone again. He doesn't seem to mind it so much. But Ellen . . . why Ellen needs you, Jan." Mrs. Mayor sighed, heaving plump shoulders and rippling plump arms. "All she thinks about is the past. What she remembers of it. For she surely doesn't remember all. Just flashes, with blank spaces between them. A trial to her, I know. And no one but him to talk to. No wonder . . . there, Jan dear, if you do go, then before you do, you must speak to Ian. You must make him see . . ."

Jan absently agreed.

But she found herself suddenly wondering if she had been mistaken. If she had convinced herself wrongly that the girl upstairs, the girl Ian was now talking to, wasn't Ellen Olney.

Thalia's death, David's death, had brought her into emotional exhaustion, into breakdown. It had affected her memory. Perhaps she had simply forgotten Beirut, forgotten the letters she had written David. Perhaps . . .

But then Jan thought of Bill. He knew that the girl upstairs wasn't Ellen. He had admitted that finally.

Bill . . .

She asked herself where he was, what he was doing. She asked herself why he didn't come down to her.

She remembered the sweetness of his kiss, his arms holding her.

"Of course," Mrs. Mayor was saying, "things aren't always what they seem to be, are they, dear?"

Jan's attention returned to the quick waterfall of words.

"No. How can they be? But I am sure, dear, you must know it yourself. Why any time now Ian will . . . he'll speak his heart to you, dear Jan. Perhaps then, perhaps you won't want to leave us."

The sweetness of Bill's kiss . . .

His arms around her . . .

Mrs. Mayor's words seemed to repeat themselves in Jan's thoughts. *Things aren't always what they seem to be.*

Jan had trusted Bill.

She had believed in him.

Because of the way he looked at her, held her. Because of the way he kissed her.

But supppose what her heart said was false.

Suppose that Bill lied . . .

Suppose the girl in the room now filled with blazing lamps to dispel the shadow of fear, was actually Ellen Olney?

"Now then, I'll be going in, Jan, dear," Mrs. Mayor was saying. "Ian will be down in just a minute. You'll pour for him, won't you? I know he'll like that. Yes, he will, dear, so do." Still trailing words, Mrs. Mayor bustled inside.

Jan clenched small fists in her lap.

She told herself that no matter who the girl upstairs finally proved to be Jan dare not leave her at Ian's mercy. No matter what Bill said, no matter how much Jan yearned to flee, Thalia, or was it Ellen? had died. And Sarah . . .

Jan rose to her feet, swept by a sense of profound fear. She wondered if she could trust Bill because of the sweetness of his kiss. But who was he? Why wouldn't he tell her? He said he had checked. Checked how? Checked with whom?

There was no Carl Ballantine. The slim young man she had seen in the pictures taken in Rome was an actor, a stranded actor that Ian had hired. But why?

Bill had said Ian had known her father years and years before. What did that mean?

Bill said the letters were the one important thing he hadn't known about.

Ellen's letters . . . written before Thalia died . . .

She had to find Bill, to ask him what he planned to do.

But when she went upstairs she heard Ian and Bill talking, their voices crossing in words she couldn't quite hear.

She went into her room. She brushed her dark curly hair, made up her face. She changed into a pale green dress, slipped on matching shoes. She glanced in the mirror. Her unsmiling face looked back at her. She told herself that she must smile. She must smile for Ian, just as she had changed for Ian. She was making time.

Ian had told her to wait on the terrace. The tea tray was ready. She would go down, and smile at him, and hope that he couldn't read her mind.

As she went down the hallway, she listened for the two blending voices, Ian's and Bill's, but she heard nothing now except the whispering silence. She thought that they would be on the terrace, waiting for her.

She moistened her dry lips.

Perhaps she would find some way of talking to Bill alone.

But the terrace was empty.

She went to the red stone wall. The sprawling meadows were pale pink under the slanting sun, as if lightly touched by the shadow of Mercer Mountain.

A pale pink cloud of dust trailed along the road below.

She glanced down at the parking area. Bill's car was gone.

She had only a moment to feel the swift hurt sinking of her heart. Then Ian said, as if taking the words from her mind, "Yes, Jan, Bill's gone."

She turned slowly. "Oh? I didn't realize that . . ."

"He asks that I make his apologies. There was, after all, nothing more for him to do here. And in the circumstances . . ." Ian shrugged massive shoulders. "He tactfully decided to withdraw. If you should have a message for him, I can deliver it. He'll call me from Denver. In about four hours, I imagine. He had agreed to do a small errand for me, if you remember."

"No," she said evenly. "I have no message for him." There was a gleam of satisfaction in Ian's blue flame eyes. She saw it, wondered at it.

Bill had pleaded for her trust, warned her, kissed her. Now he had abandoned her.

She ignored the swift sinking of her heart. She reminded herself that she was Jan Olney. She could take care of herself, and always had, and always would.

But there was a tightness in her throat. Her lips were too dry. She moistened them, then smiled at Ian. "The tea will be cold."

"Will you pour for us?"

She nodded, went to the table. She filled a cup for him, then looked at him.

He had remained in the doorway. He stood still, suntouched, his red-gold head gleaming, watching her with those hot blue eyes which suddenly seemed to see, to know, everything.

She wanted to smile at him again. She wanted to go to him, hand him the cup she held. But she seemed frozen behind an invisible barrier. She couldn't move.

He stood there, a great golden god out of an ancient myth, or like a great modern god made of splintering log and studded with rusty tin.

She thought, Bill, Bill, why did you leave me here?

And Ian's blue flame eyes seemed to flicker with hidden laughter. He came to her, took the cup she held and set it aside.

"You're thinking long thoughts if your face is a mirror," he said.

"Not really."

"Do you find it lonely here?"

"It's very beautiful, Ian."

"We wouldn't have to stay here, of course." His blue flame eyes touched her face, then slid away. "Perhaps soon."

"You're thinking about leaving?"

"I could. If there were reason to."

"But why do you need a reason, Ian?"

"For the time being, because of Ellen . . ." His deep voice trailed away.

He took Jan's hand. He took her hand gently, but she felt imprisoned by his touch. He drew her against him, and she couldn't pull back, couldn't resist. She was without will, and afraid.

His mouth came down on hers, compelling, demanding.

Bill's kiss had been sweetness, warmth.

Ian's was bitter, icy.

Yet she didn't dare pull away from him.

He must not know the revulsion that swept her.

He must still hope, still believe, that he could win her, and through her, win the Olney fortune.

He must think her so well deceived that she would marry him, become his next victim.

It was the only way that she could make time.

She remained still within the tight circle of his arms for a moment longer, still, with his demanding lips on hers. Then she turned her face aside, and smiled, feeling a blush burn her cheeks.

But his big hand settled under her chin, tipped her head back, held her. He smiled at her, and she saw mockery in his eyes before he bent to her, pressed his mouth on hers again.

It was a long, brutal kiss, a revealing kiss.

She knew what the mockery in his eyes had meant.

She had in no way been able to deceive him.

She moved within the tight circle of his arms.

He let her go instantly, still smiling down at her, "How becoming your blush is, Jan."

To cover her whirling thoughts, she went to the table, took up her cup of tea.

"Very nice," he went on softly, with an odd edge in his deep voice.

She waited, knowing that more was to come.

For she was certain now that he had decided to settle

for what David had left to Ellen. He must insist that the documents be signed. And then . . . ? Then . . . ?

He said smoothly, "Within a few minutes, Ellen will be coming down, Jan."

"Good. Then she's feeling better?"

"Hardly." The odd edge was even more noticeable.

"Oh, I'm sorry, Ian."

"Are you?" His eyes swept her in a mocking glance. "Surely you knew that your visit with her this afternoon, while I was gone, would . . ."

"I didn't mean to upset her," Jan protested quickly. Ian didn't answer.

But she knew the truth. He had taken Vera to the bus, attended Sarah Jarvis' burial service, and returned to Ballantine Lodge already knowing what he must do. He had some way or other gotten Bill to leave. So that she would be left there alone.

The game Ian had played with her was *his* game all along. He had been making time for himself. Time in which to . . .

He said, "When Ellen comes down, Jan, I would like very much for you to have the papers here. They will be signed, all taken care of, this afternoon."

Jan moistened her dry lips. "Oughtn't we to wait and see how she is?"

"I know how she will be, Jan."

Jan didn't answer him.

"Please," he said smoothly, "Please get the papers now."

She could think of no way to refuse, but still, she hesitated.

"It will be better for you, for Ellen as well, if you do as I say, Jan."

She drew a deep breath, and nodded, and went inside. As she slowly climbed the steps, she asked herself why Bill had abandoned her, what had happened. He had pleaded for her trust, warned her that once the papers were signed, Ellen would die, and she herself would die. And then he had left her, left her alone in Ballantine Lodge.

Now those papers would be signed.

It would be as Ian had intended all along. He had insisted on taking Vera in to Mercer. Had he wanted to keep the others from questioning her? Or had he simply wanted to question her further himself? Had Vera told him then that Jan had been with Sarah Jarvis, had been there when Vera thought she heard the old lady speak? Did Ian assume that Jan had been able to guess the truth? Had he decided then that the papers must be signed at once? Or had he decided that when he returned and spoke to Ellen?

Jan went along the dim silent corridor, paused before her door, then went in. Unwillingly, full of despair, she crossed the sunset-bright room to the closet.

The 'when' of it no longer mattered, she told herself.

Ian was waiting for her.

Ellen would be with him.

Jan could think of no way to stop him now.

Except . . . her hand froze on the door knob . . . except . . . yes, yes, why hadn't she thought of that before?

She must destroy the papers. Destroy them immediately. She jerked the door open, reached toward the top shelf.

Chapter 18

SHE STARED unbelievingly at the place where it should have been.

It was gone, gone.

She backed away from the closet, sent a single wild glance around the room.

Bill!

He had left her, but he had taken the folder with him.

She savored a swift sweet exulting thought. Bill had said he would help her. And he had.

She remembered his dark sober eyes, his sudden smile so full of quick awareness.

But a whisper of sound in the hall brought her to the door.

Ellen leaned at the door across from hers.

Jan heard her mumble, "Thalia. Thalia."

And Ian was waiting downstairs.

"We must go down," Jan said.

Ellen shook her golden head. "No. No. I won't," and turned, and wandered away like a sleepwalker, past the steps, and into the furthest wing.

Watching until she had disappeared, Jan asked herself why Ellen leaned at the door of Thalia's room. Was it as Ian had once told Jan? That Ellen missed Thalia, tried that way to be close to her? Or was it that Ellen, clinging to the memory of her own identity, to the memory of her identity as Thalia, sought confirmation in the room that had once been hers?

But it was no use trying to guess. Ian was waiting.

Jan went down to the terrace.

The red sunset had faded. Thick twilight spread across the mountain, across the meadows below.

Ian, his face in shadow, turned to look at her.

She paused in the doorway.

"Well?" he asked.

"It isn't there, Ian. The folder, all the papers, are gone."

She had not known what to expect, what he would do. It frightened her even more that he simply sat there, looking at her.

Then he smiled, "And what do you hope to accomplish by that?"

"I? Ian, I don't know what you're talking about."

"Don't you?" he asked softly. "Do you think I don't understand you? That I don't know what has been in your mind all along? You wrote to Ellen, then you came here to see her. Yes. It was to see her, of course. The papers could have been delivered by mail. But you came here to see her, didn't you? To see her, question her. And I know why. Because you're a true Olney. Your father all over again. You intended to strip Ellen of her inheritance if you could. Your questions . . . designed to cast doubt on her sanity. I thought I had explained her condition to you, that her memory is affected by her grief. That she has forgotten so much she can't even remember writing those poor pleading letters to David. Letters he ignored. She needed him. She needed him so. But he put his career first. He would not come to her."

Jan thought of those letters. They had been written before Thalia died, before Ellen had collapsed. Had they been written just to bring David to Ballantine Lodge?

"But it won't work, you know," Ian went on smoothly. "You didn't have time to destroy the papers while you were up in your room. And . . ." he smiled slightly, "I know that Bill didn't take them with him. I was there, watching, while he packed." Ian got to his feet, huge, hard as rock. "So . . . so they are somewhere in the house, Jan. Shall we find them now?"

It wasn't really a question, and his fingers, tight and bruising at her elbow, didn't allow her to hang back.

He drew her with him, inside the house, into the whispering silence, and then up the stairs.

"Ellen will sign those papers. Sign them soon. This time it won't be like the last. Like your father and Ballantine Wells."

She heard the open hatred in Ian's voice, and shivered.

He smiled down at her, his bruising fingers tightening.

"Ellen will sign them," he repeated.

Jan knew that Ellen would. Ian would see to that.

The girl with the wide, dazed eyes, the long golden hair, would do whatever Ian told her to.

He controlled her, just as he had controlled Sarah Jarvis. With words . . . Jan remembered Vera saying, " 'Sarah Jarvis did everything for the Ballantines always,' that's what he said, standing beside her bed." With words . . . yes. And with drugs. What words did he say to the girl that he still insisted was Ellen? And why did he continue, even now, to pretend that he hadn't guessed Jan knew the truth?

Did that mean that he wasn't sure?

That there was, after all, a chance that he might allow her, once the papers were signed, to leave?

And if he did, what of the girl with the golden hair?

Could Jan leave her with Ian in Ballantine Lodge?

"Let us save time," Ian said suddenly. "Where did you hide them?"

"I didn't, Ian."

He looked down at her.

She repeated evenly, "I tell you, I didn't hide them."

He shrugged his massive shoulders. "Then it is only a matter of a few minutes more. I will find them, you know."

His very assurance in the search told her that he must be right.

She watched him methodically examine her room, go over it slowly, carefully, replacing the mattress he had raised, re-setting the disturbed cushions of the chair, gently closing every drawer he had opened.

She tried not to think of where Bill might have hidden the folders. She knew that he had not had time to destroy it. And if he had not taken it with him, then it was somewhere, somewhere within the house, as Ian had said. If it were, then Ian would find it.

And he did.

When he was finished examining her room, he smiled at her, said, "Come along, Jan dear," and waited until she followed him down the hall to the end room.

He went in, turned on the light.

Jan hesitated on the threshold, thinking of the small waxen figure that had died on the bed there.

Jan didn't know what he was thinking when he bent over, shifted the mattress, felt under it, then straightened. She didn't know what he was thinking, but he smiled at her, and held out the folder.

"You see," he said. "A rather obvious place. But, I suppose, at the moment, you could think of none better."

"I didn't put it there," she told him.

"Never mind." He came toward her, and she backed away. She looked like a lost, frightened child, her gray eyes wide, her mouth trembling. He smiled at her again, and flipped off the light. "We'll go to Ellen now."

Jan said faintly, "You don't understand, Ian. I came here only to help Ellen. I never dreamed you would think there was any other reason."

She thought that if she could convince him of the truth of that, if he didn't know that she had guessed the truth about Sarah, about Ellen, there was still a chance that she could save herself. But once again, she thought of the girl with the golden hair, the girl who had loved David . . .

Ian looked down at Jan, amusement narrowing his eyes. "It doesn't matter. I believe that we understand each other."

She walked slowly, hanging back, he looming beside her, the folder under his arm. She walked slowly through the long dim corridor, but too soon they were at Ellen's door.

He tapped it, then went it, motioning Jan with him.

Ellen, wrapped in a green robe, huddled on the lounge. She raised her golden head, blinked swollen eyes, when he turned on the lamp beside her.

"It's just a small thing for you to do, Ellen," he said gently. "You see, Jan has decided that she wants to leave tomorrow. So now . . . Well, here you are . . . the papers. They cover what David has left you, Ellen. You must sign them, so that Jan can leave."

"But I don't want Jan to go," Ellen protested. "No. I can't." She burst into tears. "I loved David so. I can't . . . I can't . . ."

Ian's big hand fell on her shoulder. He shook her lightly. "That will do, Ellen. Do you want Jan to think that you're completely mad?" His voice hardened. "Or do you want her to think even worse?" He moved a table closer to the weeping girl, put the folder on it, took out a pen. "Jan," he said, without looking at her, "if you'll just come here, explain . . ."

It was done, done in an unbelievably few moments, while Ian stood over Ellen and Jan, watching.

The stack of papers, signed, the ink dry . . .

Ian separated them, shuffled them. "Copies for you, Jan. And these for us, of course . . ."

She nodded, accepted what he handed her, thanked him.

In an even voice, she thanked him as he gave her the papers that were her death warrant. That might be Ellen's as well.

He said, "Now that this is done, I imagine that you'll want to pack. I'll arrange that the train be flagged for a stop in Mercer. That will be in the morning, of course."

She nodded, wondering if morning would ever come, and as she left the room, Ellen cried, "No, Ian. No," before he closed the door, sealing her protest away.

Jan hurried to her room, clutching the folder to her. There, frightened into a strange vague numbness, she flung it on the bed. Pictures, papers, spilled from it.

The pictures . . . Carl, who didn't exist . . .

Thalia, smiling with love, at David . . .

Ellen and David together . . .

Ellen and Thalia together . . . the one smiling at David, the other looking at Ian . . .

One with a heart of stone. One with a heart of love . . .

Jan gathered the pictures. She took up the papers, smoothed them, looked at them. All signed now. Ellen Ballantine Olney.

She flipped the pages idly. Ellen Ballantine Olney. Ellen Ballantine Olney. Thalia Ballantine Olney. Thalia . . .

Jan gasped. Thalia . . . Thalia Ballantine Olney . . . Yes, it was written there, written neatly in the same ink, by the hand.

The girl with the long golden hair, the girl Jan had always known as Ellen, had tried to warn her, had written her own name, had written Thalia . . .

Jan quickly shuffled the papers together, replaced them in the folder, and then, with sinking heart, remembered the copies that Ian had.

Some time he would look at them.

Some time he would know.

But what could she do?

She looked wildly around the room.

There was no escape.

There was no one to help her.

Jan stood at the window, dressed, waiting.

The hours had moved slowly.

She and Ian had had dinner together, Mrs. Mayor twittering nervously around them.

Ian asked, "Are you packed, Jan?" and Jan nodded.

Mrs. Mayor cried, "Oh, are you leaving, Jan, dear? Are you? But I thought . . . Oh, dear . . . I am sorry. I . . ."

Ian cut in smoothly, "Jan finds us rather depressing, I'm afraid." He smiled at Jan. "Haven't you noticed that, Mrs. Mayor."

The older woman's plump face wrinkled in bewilderment. "Well, in the last few days, it has been . . . I mean, you have looked rather peaked, Jan, dear. But I did think . . . oh, I am sorry." Her round blue eyes shifted away from Jan. "We will miss you . . ." she murmured as she bustled out of the room.

"Depressing," Ian said softly. "This house . . . the Ballantine curse."

"I told you. I don't believe in curses," Jan said evenly.

But she thought that in a way he was right. The curse of greed lay upon him.

She glanced around the big room, the room so marked by transience that it seemed hardly possible anyone had ever lived there.

He had come there, with Sarah, with Thalia, as soon as he returned home. He had bought the isolated house, and settled there, as if the Ballantines had owned it for years.

It had been, always, a part of what he planned to do. But what had he planned then? Ellen, with David in Beirut . . . Ellen, coming back . . . then pleading with David to join her . . .

A faint flicker of light danced in the darkness below, then faded.

Jan leaned closer to the window, staring at the spot where it had been. But it was gone, not repeated.

Silver moonlight slowly spread a thin glow across the terrace.

The house slowly settled into whispering silence.

And Jan waited, waited for the chance that might not come, waited for the morning that might not come.

And suddenly, below her, on the moonlit terrace, there was movement. A shadow fell, big and black, across the silvered stone, across the white leatherette chair from which a black coil had risen to strike at her.

A shadow moved to the red stone wall, and stood there for a moment, and then turned, an arm raised, beckoning.

Ian, with his red-gold head a glowing nimbus, and his face shadowed, with his arm raised, calling her soundlessly through the night.

But she would not go to him.

She would not go.

She stood very still, while long moments passed.

She watched him stand there, a god out of an ancient myth, but silvered now. A god of evil, as heartless as that man-made thing of splintered wood and brass studs that stood in the center of Mercer's square.

She watched him stand there, and then, with a gasp of terror, she saw the shadows stir, and break and reform, and Ellen stepped out into the moonlight.

She moved like a sleepwalker, trailing the silver gray robe that looked like a single tear drop.

Ian turned to her, opened his arms, and drew her with him to the terrace wall.

Jan realized then that Ian had not been beckoning to her, but to Ellen. It was Ellen that he had called to come down to him. Ellen . . .

Jan spun away from the window. She fought her door open, flung herself into the darkness of the hallway. She raced down the steps, straining for a sound from outside, for a cry, a scream.

But there was nothing, nothing.

She reached the foyer, and ran across it, and somewhere, off in the living room, she thought she glimpsed a moving shadow. But she didn't dare stop.

Ian had called Ellen down to him, and drawn her with him to the terrace wall.

Jan had to stop him. To stop him before . . .

The door was wide open.

Looking beyond it, she could see the silver-lit terrace, but the wall was empty now.

She sensed her danger. It was too late to stop, to turn back. Her headlong flight took her on, outside, and into Ian's arms.

He held her close, close in a lover's embrace, and whispered words she couldn't understand. He held her, drew her towards the empty wall.

She struggled against his strength. She cried, "What did you do with Ellen, Ian?"

"I sent her inside," he said gently. "Now that she's served her purpose, I sent her inside. She oughtn't to be wandering alone in the night, Jan. She can't be trusted, you know. My poor sister . . ."

Jan fought his iron grip, kicked and clawed, and tried to scream. But he held her, held her easily, one big hand over her mouth, gagging her, the other twisting her arm cruelly behind her. He moved her that way, crushing her against him, until he had her at the wall, and pressed her against it, the stone gouging her thighs and ribs, tearing at her as the red ridges below would tear at her when he flung her over to fall on them.

"Brave, brave Jan," he whispered, in open mockery. "A true Olney to the last. My decoy brought you down as I never could. My decoy . . . poor Ellen. You came to save her, didn't you, Jan?"

He released her for an instant.

She drew a breath, a scream building in her throat. But it strangled behind her lips. She had only that instant of freedom before he seized her again. An arm behind her, swinging her up, an arm holding her, her face pressed into the angle of his shoulder, breath gone, scream strangled.

She still fought him, struggled against his overpowering strength, and knew that the swift silent fight was useless. She was up, moving in empty air. She went limp. She clung to him. Leech-like, she clung to his body, and she felt him stagger, and jerk back, and suddenly, she was free, falling.

She hit the edge of the wall. She fell to her knees, pain-blinded, and dizzy, and so near to fainting that the silver terrace seemed black, black with moving shadows, with struggling shadows.

She forced herself to her feet, clung to the wall. In that moment, she knew who had saved her, how he had saved her.

And Ian cried out, "But you called. You called me from Denver!"

"Not I, Ian. That was a friend of mine," Bill answered, and rose, and stepped back.

Jan wondered that Ian lay so unmoving, up on one elbow now, his mouth bloody and twisted, but so carefully unmoving.

Then she saw the gun in Bill's fist, and she understood.

But in that same moment, too, Ellen appeared in the doorway. Her hair was cut short, hacked away, and hung around her tilted head. Like a sleepwalker, she moved into the sunlight.

"Ellen," Bill cried in warning.

"No. Thalia," she whispered, and moved between Bill and Ian. "I'm Thalia. Ellen. Ellen. Ellen. That's what he kept saying to me. Ellen. So that I almost forgot who I am. But I'm Thalia." She stood over Ian. "No more," she said. "It doesn't matter." She turned, looked dreamily at Jan. "Do you understand? It was always, always the Olneys."

Ian said harshly, "Be quiet, Ellen. Ellen, I tell you, you must be quiet."

She looked down at him. "I told you. It doesn't matter any more. I'm not afraid any more. I'm Thalia, and I'm not afraid." She looked at Jan again. "The Olneys . . . all those years. First it was just Ian. But then Ellen . . . Ellen too. And he found out about David, you see. He knew about David, and he took us all to Rome. Sarah, and Ellen, and me. And he found Carl there. It was such a good family group. That's how Ian's mind works, you know. He plans . . . he plans ahead so far. David . . . if he had loved me . . . married me . . . then . . ." Thalia shrugged slim shoulders, and the gown rippled around her, brushed Ian's arm. "But David loved Ellen, and married her. Just as Ian planned, of course. We came back here, and waited those few months, and then Ellen returned. That was planned, too."

"Be quiet," Ian said again.

"But it's over," she answered in an odd, dreaming voice. "Can't you understand that? It's all over. Jan knows. Bill knows. It's all over, Ian."

Jan realized that Thalia was too close to Ian, bending near him, talking to him, and cried out.

But it was too late.

Ian was up, on his feet. His arms were around Thalia, crushing her to him. As he backed away, holding her, he said thinly, "Shoot now, Bill," and grinned.

Bill lowered the gun. He sent a swift, sober glance at Jan, a warning glance.

And Thalia, moving willingly within the tight circle of Ian's arms, said gently, dreamily, "But it doesn't matter, Ian. It's all over."

"You won't get far," Bill told him.

"Then shoot now," Ian grinned. His blue flame eyes raked Jan. "We were close. Close to it, I tell you. Like that time with Ballantine Wells."

He had backed to the top of the stone stairs. He still held Thalia before him.

He reached for the step behind him, moved down, and Thalia said, "I loved David, you know. That's why I killed Ellen. She came home. She wrote the letters to bring him back here, so that Ian could . . . Well, I couldn't let it happen. I told her. We fought. And she fell. I had to be Ellen then. At least until David came. That's what Ian made me do. Be Ellen. For just until David came. Otherwise Ian would have told. And somehow, David died. You came instead, Jan. And Sarah . . . poor Sarah who had tried to protect me . . . Ian? Why? Why?"

He had reached for the second step. He had tipped back, slightly unbalanced by the weight of Thalia in his arms.

She suddenly lashed out at him.

Her slight body arched against him, thrusting, thrusting . . .

They seemed to hang on the steps, both wrapped in her silken robe. They hung there, wavering for a long icy moment.

Jan started forward, her small hands out and reaching.

Bill lunged across the distance.

But they were both too late.

Ian shouted, and Thalia crumpled into him, and still wrapped in her silken robe, they overbalanced and fell backward together into the silver shadows of the steep stone steps.

The sounds of the fall made long long echoes that finally faded into the whispering silence of the house.

Jan listened, and listening, wept, while Bill quickly disappeared into the silvery darkness below.

Later, when the police had come and gone, when the explanations had been made, and what had to be done was done, and Mrs. Mayor, twittering nervously, had been put on a bus for Omaha, and the keys of Ballantine Lodge turned over to the wizened drug store proprietor in town, then Bill would put Jan into his car, and drive her away forever from the shadow of Mercer Mountain.

He would explain that he was a State Department investigator, working out of the Consulate in Beirut. He had discovered, even before David's death, the link between the Olneys and Ballantines in South America, and learned, too, that though the Ballantines lived as if they were wealthy they had very little traceable income. Suspicious that Ellen had left David so soon after their marriage, Bill decided, when David died, to continue his investigation, and found, when he arrived at Ballantine Lodge, that Thalia was impersonating Ellen. Before he knew what was happening, or why, before he had any proof he could use against Ian and Thalia, Jan had arrived. He had felt that ignorance was her greatest protection against Ian. Then Sarah was murdered, and Jan told him that she was certain Ellen was an impostor. He had sent her down to talk to Ian, hidden the folder, knowing there was no time then to destroy it. Just a few minutes later, Ian had politely, but bluntly, told Bill that he was expected to leave, and stayed with Bill while he packed, and until he had driven away. Bill was willing enough to have Ian think he was gone, but left the car hidden in the cedars, circled back to the house on foot, and hidden himself, awaiting a chance to find Jan, take her away. Instead, Ian had come out into the moonlight . . . And Jan, listening, would remember David's feverish questions, and wince, but then be grateful that he had never known the truth.

All that came later, in bright sunshine, with the shadow of Mercer Mountain falling away behind them . . .

Now Jan listened to the fading echoes, and wept.

When she at last raised her head, Bill was coming up the steps toward her.

He said soberly, "She loved David. That was the last thing she told me."

"And Ian?" Jan whispered.

Bill shook his dark head slowly.

Then he opened his arms wide, and she ran to him to be comforted.